THE SOCIETY OF LIGHT

Volume 1

The Compendium Of Alchemists' Abstruse Contrivances

Part 1

DOMINIC DANVERS

Tom and Zoe

CHAPTER 1

1945

It was dark, so very dark. The air was thick with moisture and Henry could hardly see the distant lights flickering across the London skyline as he ran. The gravel crunched beneath his heavy footsteps.

He kept close to the palace wall. Below were the sloping verges and thick trees of the park. It was safer to remain on high ground and hope they would not climb from the city below.

He felt the chill of frosty cold air at the nape of his neck. It ran through his body down to his toes until he could not run any longer.

Henry found himself at the East Court entrance to the palace. Looking up, he made out the huge coloured stained-glass rose towering above him and next to it, the mezzanine. That was it!

Henry pushed at the large entrance doors. They were locked.

He edged nervously along the high walls looking for a way in. Tucked into a small corner, Henry found a steel joist protruding through the outer wall and above a service ladder.

It required fine balance and a bit of luck but Henry was naturally nimble and he stepped onto the joist and launched himself upward in one movement managing to grab the ladder and pull himself up. He climbed the ladder and needed only to jump over the parapet wall to find himself on the mezzanine.

The mezzanine was covered in old rubble. The palace had seen better days and this particular part of the building was run down and crumbling in parts.

Henry looked back and forth trying to identify the silhouettes of ancient symbols carved into the stonework. The silhouettes were worn by time and the elements and this made it almost impossible to distinguish between them. He needed to find Bastet (the Egyptian goddess of protection) depicted by a cat. If he could make contact with the silhouette, it should at least afford him the time to relay his findings back to the Society.

Henry squinted and peered through the fog searching for her. A clearing in the mist revealed Bastet's form at the end of the mezzanine, seemingly moving in the moonlight as if given life.

Henry lurched forward but this time his instinctive athleticism betrayed forethought and his foot caught the rubble sending him tumbling to the floor. His head struck the cold stone and Henry winced in pain before passing out.

He awoke minutes later to a ringing in his ears. At first, Henry thought the ringing to be a result of the fall but gradually the noise increased in volume and he realised it wasn't coming from inside his head but around him.

They had climbed the verge and wall and slowly emerged onto the mezzanine. Henry desperately craned his neck towards Bastet and stretched his arms towards her as the mist thickened obscuring his vision until eventually he saw... and felt nothing.

CHAPTER 2

Tom

Tom bounced down the stairs excited by the prospect of making new friends.

He was a very outgoing and enthusiastic child. One would think this would make it easier for him to bond with other children but often they felt intimidated by his zeal and backed away.

But this was a new school with new children. His father had taken on a new role in London.

Tom's family came from the Shetland Islands which lies one hundred and seventy miles north of the Scottish mainland. Its Norse name being Hjaltland. They had lived there for as long as Tom could remember until moving to London.

Tom's father was a geologist. His job had taken him all over the world and he had recently taken the seat as head of geology at University College London. Tom hoped that this move would mean his father would finally settle in one place with his family.

His mother was a professional carer. She had started work in the local home for the retired and elderly. She loved dearly and was dearly loved in return. The home was delighted to have her. She was radiant and her presence changed those who met her, unknown to them, always and forever.

Tom often wondered how he had come to be born and grow up with his mother and father in the Shetland Islands. One's origin was something most children accepted without question but not Tom. He had never quizzed his parents directly on the subject. He felt it would offend them. But having moved from his birthplace, Tom now needed to know.

Tom's family history on the islands could be traced back centuries to the time of Norsemen - the Vikings.

Leaving his old school wasn't much of a strain. He had never really settled there. The teachers found him overbearing and didn't quite know how to cope with his inquisitive nature. Tom was full of questions about this and that. So much so that he earned himself a reputation as a great distraction and was constantly being told to pipe down.

Tom never quite understood why he shouldn't be inquisitive and question everything. Surely, that was the point of learning? But the teachers found it too much. Perhaps they needed to be as enthusiastic as Tom.

In the classroom, the children found him amusing. They were delighted that Tom took up so much time with his constant interruptions so they could avoid having to work.

In the playground though, it was different. To the children, Tom was seen as just simply annoying. A 'know it all' who tried too hard to befriend.

Tom found himself isolated but it wasn't in his nature to allow it to slow him down. He was a very confident child who took enormous joy in being. Every day was a great adventure and opportunity for discovery. It was Tom's driving force which would carry him forward in life.

Tom was truly fearless; not in the sense that he was brave (that he felt fear but overcame it) but that Tom's yearning to discover clouded better judgment. He would never fear anything. All he would ever want was to understand everything. To do so, Tom needed friends to look out for him.

Tom had no appetite for breakfast. He was itching to leave the house and run at full tilt to the school gates. Mum had left for work, a schoolteacher herself, and dad called out from the shower,

"Go Tom. Be brave and have fun!"

Dad knew his son well. He knew that Tom struggled to make friends and it was not a question of courage or encouragement, but of support which he felt would give Tom that extra confidence to secure friendship. Tom deserved it. He was a kind-hearted and benevolent boy. He would learn soon enough that those traits were admirable but could put him in harm's way.

Tom left the house at pace.

His dad heard the door slam as Tom tore up the street. The house was one block from the school and Tom ran into a mêlée at the school gates.

He sensed the emotions of the crowd as if they were floating around him. It was overwhelming. Tom had never felt like it before. His head whirled and he found himself sapped of energy as he staggered and dropped to the ground.

But as he did so, a hand grabbed his arm so hard that it hurt. He looked up and was blinded by a shock of red hair,

"Are you OK?", Tom heard.

"I'm Zoe, what's your name?".

"Tom", Tom said.

"I'm pleased to meet you Tom. Can we be friends?", Zoe asked.

And there it began, again.

CHAPTER 3

Zoe

"Get off me!", Zoe screamed.

The nurse struggled to make the suture. Zoe had a gash to her forehead from the fall and it needed to be closed.

"Stay still!", the nurse declared in frustration.

"No!", Zoe retorted angrily.

"Get off me, you cow!", Zoe cried, "I don't need stitches, it's just a scratch. Get that needle away from me!".

Like Tom, Zoe was very confident. Unlike Tom, Zoe had little interest in learning and much more interest in dictating her view of the world to those around her. This resulted in several serious skirmishes in a multitude of schools and expulsions.

Zoe didn't care about the opinions of others and no teacher could change that. Her view of life was clear and absolute. It was her way or no way at all.

Zoe was born ready for anything. She was adopted at birth and had a wonderful upbringing despite her high jinks' tendencies.

Zoe's adopted parents were both secondary school teachers. They were trained in managing challenging children but dealing with one's own child was very different, and Zoe was certainly no exception to that rule!

Both her parents came from Cornwall - her father from Falmouth and her mother from Penzance.

Zoe's parents had recognised her inclination towards the 'daring' and 'bold' from infancy. They realised quickly that this was an integral part of her nature and being insightful they chose to allow it in a controlled and responsible fashion hoping that in time it would allow her to get ahead in life.

Zoe's fiery red hair befitted her character and temperament. She had a very warm heart (like Tom) but a very short temper. Most children at school tended to steer clear of her, confused by her friendly discourse one minute and sharp rebuke the next. They were probably right to do so.

The few who stuck with her were rewarded with unprecedented acts of such charity and devotion. Becoming Zoe's friend was akin to taking a blood oath. She expected complete loyalty in return. It was rather oppressive.

Zoe continued to protest to the nurse and Zoe's mother looked on, perplexed. She had never been able to control Zoe.

"Zoe! Stay still and let the nurse do her job. She is only trying to help you!", her mother pleaded.

But Zoe ignored her mother's plea. She had never liked hospitals, let alone needles.

Eventually, the nurse gave up and resigned herself to applying a gauze. The wound wouldn't heal as well but at least it would stay clean. Zoe relaxed slightly as the nurse finished the job.

"Another scar", the nurse said with a sigh. "You certainly have a fine collection. When are you going to slow down and stop being so reckless Zoe? You're going to really hurt yourself one day."

"Never!", Zoe retorted. "Life is too short."

Coming from a sixteen years' old, that was a remarkable statement.
Zoe like Tom was driven by a desire to live life to the full but for her that involved taking risks, mostly physical. Zoe was incredibly athletic for her age and set herself physical challenges every day.

Todays was leaping the divide between garden walls. The gap was some twelve feet. From a standing position, that was a tall order for an adult let alone an adolescent. Zoe had narrowly missed the neighbour's wall. Her foot had slipped from the edge of the wall top which then received her brow in quick succession.

Zoe's mother had only noticed Zoe from the kitchen window as she climbed back onto their garden wall to give it another go, blood dripping from her forehead.

Zoe would never give up on anything, or anyone to whom she took a liking, for that matter.

She left the hospital and returned home with her mother in the car. Zoe remained silent all the way home, scheming how she could get back out into the garden without her mother noticing in order to attempt the jump again.

She was returning to school the next day after the summer break and her mother was determined that Zoe had a good night's sleep. She enticed her with take away pizza and the promise she could eat it in her room.

By the time they arrived home the sun was setting. Perhaps she would wait until tomorrow, Zoe pondered. She needed to be alert and ready to take on the teachers tomorrow and the opportunity to lock herself away in her room would give her time to plan her next dare without her parents bothering her about the holiday homework she hadn't even started. And Zoe could never refuse pizza.

Zoe was to discover that her parents had done just the right thing in allowing her to develop her somewhat physical skills. She would need them for who she was soon to become.

She hoped to meet someone different at school this term and she would. But she wouldn't know how different he was, at least for a short while.

CHAPTER 4

New Beginnings

Madame Vauqelin came from a long line of Wardens dating back to the medieval times. Vauqelin was a translation of the German name 'Walchelin' which was derived from the ancient Germanic word 'Walha' meaning foreigner. Wardens had always been selected from outside the Society. Their allegiance was unwavering and their judgment impartial.

Despite the Germanic origin of her name, Madame Vauqelin was undoubtedly French. She had an implacable sense of right and wrong and was, above all, a cynic and supreme critic. These attributes, she hoped privately, would always keep her children safe. It would keep the Society safe.

She moved through the Great Hall at speed. The signs were there and there was no time to lose.

Madame struck the doors with her staff three times and they opened.

Beyond the doors, in the Chamber, sat the Assembly. Eight elected Emissaries and painted on the ceiling the sign of Eight.

On the stone floor was carved the eight-pointed windrose.

They sat on cathedrae (ceremonial chairs) at the end of each of the eight points. Each cathedra was different, some very plain and some very ornate.

Above each point, on the walls, were engraved the names of the principal winds.

The Cardinal Winds: -
North - Tramontane
South - Ostro
East - Levante
West - Ponente

The Ordinal Winds: -
Northeast - Grecale
Northwest - Maestro
Southeast - Sirocco
Southwest - Libeccio

The windrose was a compass and across its lines lay the eight key landmarks.

At its centre was Corum (located 150km south-east of the Turkey capital Ankarra) believed by the Society to mark the centre point of the earth. This has long been debated (even within the Society). Some believed the centre to be at the Great Pyramid of Giza in Egypt and others the Ka'bah of Mecca in Saudi Arabia or The Dome of the Rock in Jerusalem.

Madame stood at the centre of the windrose.

"Why have you summoned us?", Emissary Tramontane enquired.

Madame drew a long and deep breath. The Assembly had only met three times in the last century and traditionally avoided being in the same place at the same time. The last time the Assembly met was in 1945 following the passing of Custodian Henry and the election of his successor. A matter of utmost urgency was required to convene a full meeting and Madame knew this was such a matter.

"It has begun.", she said firmly.

"How so?", Emissary Tramontane replied.

"I have located the boy and he has already been united with the girl.", Madame said.

"Where?", replied Emissary Tramontane.

"In London.", Madame confirmed.

"How can that be possible?", Emissary Ostro interjected, "The prophecy is quite clear on the timing. Only once every quarter millennium. It can't be. It's far too soon!"

CHAPTER 5

The Red Lodestone

The Society had been founded in the late part of the eleventh century in Greenwich or Grenewych as it was known then (meaning 'green settlement') by mariners but its roots dated back much earlier.

Mariners were the source of many strange tales from land and sea. Most had been translated innumerable times across continents until the original tale was unrecognisable and most were the fabrication of men who were determined to tell the greatest tale, even if it were a lie.

Few were as educated and cultured as the master mariners. Their experience of the world was second to none and consequently they possessed an encyclopaedic knowledge.

Master mariners were, for the most part, naval officers who knew that their job put them at great risk.

The qualification of master mariner allowed them to continue after their service to the Crown, should they be fortunate to survive, as captains of commercial vessels.

Their reputation preceded them as men of honour and integrity and the tales they told were not exaggerated.

But no tale for the mariner was more peculiar than the tale of the Red Lodestone.

Lodestone is a mineral with a magnetic quality. Pieces of suspended lodestone were used by the ancient mariners as compasses and its name was derived from Middle English meaning leading stone. Traditionally, the lodestone was a dark brown or black colour.

The Red Lodestone was discovered by Captain Richard Maynard on his travels to the West Indies in 1756.

The captain was a prolific adventurer who had travelled further than any of his fellow voyagers. He was the son of Commander Robert Maynard who caught the infamous pirate Edward "Blackbeard" Teach after the bloody battle of Okracoke Island just off the coast of North Carolina on 22nd November 1718.

The captain had bought the stone from a peddler at the port of Calicut in India.

Its colour had immediately caught the captain's eye. It was a brilliant red unlike anything he had ever seen before, almost flesh like. Ingrained within the stone were fine streaks of jet black running this way and that.

The captain was very familiar with Lodestone but the unique colour of this stone disguised its true identity.

It was about 2cm wide and 1cm thick at its centre with a natural sheen and rough to the touch.

Stones were as common at port markets as the supposed curses that were made upon them. The greater the sense of mystery, the great the price, even for the most ordinary of rocks.

The captain carried the stone with him in his coat pocket over the next few days while the ship was docked. It was not intended as a good luck charm.

The captain was not a superstitious man. He was a man of science. His tendency to apply common sense to all he encountered and avoid the trappings of myth led him to places no mariner before had ventured.

He used the stone to turn in his hands. It helped him think more clearly.

It was only when the captain held the stone next to his compass back onboard and he noticed it interfered with the dial that he realised it was magnetic like the black Lodestones he had seen before.

What was this and why was it red? he asked himself, not knowing that the stone was changing him slowly in ways he could not perceive.

CHAPTER 6

The Unity

Tom was immediately enchanted. Zoe's red hair filled the sky as he rose to his feet. Parents and kids manoeuvred around them preoccupied.

"Are you OK?", Zoe asked.

Tom was still disoriented. Principally, by the overpowering sensation he had felt at the school gates, but also by Zoe's presence. It was as if she were meant to be there at that particular moment.

"I'm OK", Tom replied. "Thank you for helping me."

"Let's go", Zoe said.

She held his hand very tightly as she led him into the school.

I know you, Tom thought. Maybe he had met Zoe before, but he did not know how much they would achieve together after today.

Zoe strode through the throng of parents and children with Tom in tow. Tom was feeling very nauseous from his collapse, but Zoe's grip was reassuring and somehow familiar to him.

They reached the main building and to its left the school infirmary. Zoe opened the door and was greeted by Miss Reynolds, part-time Biology teacher and part-time nurse.

"Zoe, we've barely started the new school term", Miss Reynolds exclaimed, "what have you done to yourself now?".

"It's not me, it's Tom", Zoe replied. "He fell outside the school gate."

"I'm OK", Tom squeaked. "Just a little nauseous."

"Sit down here Tom", Miss Reynolds said in a comforting tone. "I'll get you a glass of water. It's your first day today isn't Tom? It can be daunting. You're probably just anxious."

But Tom knew this sensation was different to anything he had felt before. It was as if he had been living in someone else's skin if only for a split second.

"Are you in pain anywhere?", Miss Reynolds enquired.

"No, not really…", Tom paused to correct himself. "Actually, now you mention it my arm isn't hurting but it feels very numb."

"Let's take a look", Miss Reynolds said.

Tom took off his jumper and extended his right arm.

"That's some tattoo, Tom!" Miss Reynolds stated.

"I don't have a tattoo." Tom replied looking down.

"Yes, you do." Miss Reynolds retorted.

Tom couldn't believe it. Running down the top of his arm from his shoulder to his elbow was a black inked compass. It had eight points in the form of arrows, but the north point was emboldened. At its centre was what looked like an eye.

"Wow, Tom, where did you get that?" Zoe asked.

Tom didn't reply. Instead, he gazed down at the tattoo in a trance.

"Tom, Tom!!" Zoe shouted.

"Yes?" Tom said.

"Where have you been? We've been calling your name for the last couple of minutes." Zoe said worryingly.

"What do you mean? I've just sat down." Tom said unsure of himself.

"I think you should probably go to A&E to have a full check-up." Miss Reynolds said. "And cover up that tattoo. They're not allowed in school Tom. You're too young anyhow. Whatever were your parents thinking!"

"What tattoo?" Tom replied.

CHAPTER 7

A Couple of Minutes

Tom's mind was filled with white smoke and the screams of men. He could smell something acrid in the air.

He glanced forward, and in the distance, saw the bow of a huge ship with the face of a beautiful siren moving closer. Around him men ran left and right, gathering up rope and pushing a huge wooden boom. Above the boom, an enormous mast flapped in the wind. It was white in colour, as far as Tom could make out, with a red and blue crest.

"Hard to starboard!" someone seemingly standing immediately next to him shouted and he felt himself lurch to the right.

"Keep that boom down!" the voice cried. "Don't let it lift!"

"Now, fire!" the voice screamed.

Then followed a rally of large explosions as orange light appeared below.

Tom noticed that the other ship was no longer ahead of him but immediately to his left. But he could not make out the movement of shadows on board. They seemed to be flitting from left to right but did not make a sound. Their silence was extremely menacing.

Next, he heard a burst of thunder, splintering of wood and screams. The noise was deafening. He heard a whizzing close to his ear and more splintering of wood behind him.

Something fell hard with a thud at his feet.

He looked down and through a clearing of smoke saw a bloodied face lying next to his feet. Tom wanted to step back but could not (as if he were occupying someone else's body without any physical control and seeing everything through their eyes).

Tom realised that he was not in his usual black converse and jeans but instead loose hanging trousers and tired black leather boots which rose to his knees. Attached to his waist was a belt from which hung two sabres and two muskets. A long overcoat covered a sullied top and another belt ran horizontally across his torso to which an exceptionally large knife with a curved blade was attached. Long, tangled, and greasy hair fell across his face.

He was standing on the top deck gripping the ship's wheel.

The wheel was made from a red coloured wood and inlaid with brass. Eight handles protruded from the outer circle. Within lay an inner circle along the top of which the words 'Bene Facitis' were inscribed and along the bottom the words 'Et Defendat'.

Tom saw himself drive the wheel sharply to the right and downwards to the deck as he felt the ship veer suddenly to the left again. The ship rose above the waves as the waters crashed and ran across the deck below.

Some sailors had tied themselves to the two masts and the bulwarks of the ship with rope and were clinging on for dear life whilst others slid about, and some were thrown overboard.

The ship crashed into its counterpart. Both ships seemed immense.

Tom could not see the bilge below but the helm on which he stood was housed some 150 feet from the floor of the hull. The bow to stern measured some 500 feet and aft to starboard 150 feet.

The ship was a stellaris galleon class. The largest of all sea vessels.

"A l'abordage!" Tom screamed the traditional battle cry.

First, some hundred men lunged forward with muskets and fired simultaneously at the shadows aboard the other ship. They dropped back and others behind ran forward with grappling hooks attached to rope which they launched across the water hooking the other ship. They pulled the ropes tight, drawing the two ships closer, and then they fastened the ropes to the bulwark. Then both sets of men clambered onto the bulwark and launched themselves across to the other ship as they disappeared into the smoke in a din of yelling, clanging of sabres and cracking of musket fire.

Tom and a reserve complement of men on the deck below watched on. Gradually, the din tapered, and Tom could hear individual voices of his crew desperately pleading for their lives until finally there was complete silence.

CHAPTER 8

Home and Away

Tom arrived home just as his mother pulled into the drive.

"Darling, how was your day?" she said, as she opened the car door.

Tom ran over to give her a hug. Mum wrapped her arms around Tom and he instantly felt lifted. Despite being his mother, she had the most restorative effect on him. He felt healed by his mother's touch.

"Come on, sweetheart", she said. "Let us go indoors and have some tea. You can tell me all about it."

Tom sat at the kitchen table as his mother prepared some toast with marmalade – Tom's favourite. Just then, Tom's dad returned. He walked into the kitchen and could see Tom was looking a little pale.

"Tough first day?" he enquired as he gave Tom a kiss on the head.

"A strange one, dad." Tom replied wearily. Dad and mum sat down next to Tom as mum said, "Start from the beginning, darling."

Tom described his encounter with Zoe and his trip to the infirmary. Then, he explained his visions on board the ship. His parents listened attentively. When Tom had finished his account, he rolled up his sleeve to reveal the tattoo.

"Goodness me, Tom. That is very impressive, my boy", his dad said. "I've always wanted a tattoo!" he sniggered. His mother looked at her husband and raised her eyebrows in disdain and said "You must be exhausted. Why don't you lie down and get some rest, sweetheart? I'll come up in a while to see you."

Tom wandered upstairs to his bedroom. As he climbed the stairs, he noted how calm his parents appeared hearing his story. He thought he had sounded utterly delirious recounting this fantastical tale, but they seemingly accepted everything Tom had told them without interjection or question – including the tattoo. That was a little odd, Tom concluded.

Tom could not sleep that night. He tossed and turned pondering the day's events and his visions. He could not rid his mind of them.

Where had he been during that time Zoe and Miss Reynolds had been calling his name? It seemed so lifelike, so real.

The smells were still so pungent and the sounds so resonant as if he were still on board the ship.

The clamour of battle rang in his ears. He had been there. He had been part of it. Tom was certain but how could that be? He had been sitting in the infirmary whilst it had all unfolded.

The temperature in the room dropped suddenly as the room began to rock forwards and backwards as it filled with mist. Tom felt very uneasy and closed his eyes to try to stop the hallucination but when he reopened them he was once again aboard the ship. It was daytime.

Tom was once again standing on the bridge looking down at the deck below.

The masts were flapping in the wind. They were ragged and torn but Tom could clearly make out the red and blue crest sown into each of them.

The design was a blue inverted V with three red hands open upward. Two on top either side of the V and one below in between the V. It depicted the crest of the house of Maynard.

Tom moved forward (or rather Captain Maynard) moved forward and descended the steps from the bridge to the lower deck.

There were very few men on board compared to Tom's last vision. The men were carrying out a variety of tasks. Some were treating the injured, others were repairing the shattered bulwarks and rigging, others were simply sat hunched on the deck.

It appeared to be the morning after the battle Tom had witnessed in his previous vision.

Captain Maynard positioned himself at the beam. He removed his cocked bicorn hat with blue and red plumage. He placed his right foot on the capstan, cleared his throat which and then spoke,

"Last night we faced pure evil and prevailed. We lost many of the crew, family, and friends but we cleared the path to our future. For today, we will find sanctuary with new family and friends. Keep an open mind and true heart because ahead lies our destiny."

Loud cheering came from all around the ship as the sailors threw their caps into the air and from the crow's nest a voice bellowed, "land ahoy!"

With that, Tom felt himself floating upwards and out of the

body of Captain Maynard.

He saw the ship growing smaller and smaller below him as he rose into the sky. On the horizon, beyond the waves, he saw an island glimmering in the sunshine. Then the light faded slowly as his vision ended.

He came around and looked up at his bedroom door. It was open - but at a very strange angle – not entirely or slightly but somewhere in between, making the void unsettling. He could see the corridor beyond his bedroom but could not see his cat Lucy who sat beyond the door against the radiator.

But Lucy could hear Tom and his breathing, however slight… anywhere and always. She had sensed the increase in his heartbeat and body temperature brought about by his visionary state. She knew Tom had not been merely dreaming and that everything he had experienced had been real albeit seen through the eyes of Captain Maynard.

Lucy joined Tom and lay at the foot of his bed. She let out a comforting purr and Tom fell fast asleep.

Tom would soon come to realise soon that Lucy was not the pretty little thing she appeared. She was Freya, one of the Great Cats, his protector, and he was the great north wind.

CHAPTER 9

Old and New

The eight Emissaries of the Society came from different parts of the globe as indicated by their respective points of the compass.

First were the Cardinals:

North (Tramontane) was of Viking origin. He represented the Winter season and Earth element.

South (Ostro) was of African origin. She represented the summer season and Fire element.

East (Levante) was of Chinese origin. He represented the Spring season and Air element.

West (Ponente) was of Native American origin. She represented the Autumn season and Water element.

Second (but by no means least) were the Ordinals. The Ordinals combined the characteristics and power of their closest Cardinals: -

Northeast (Grecale) was of Siberian origin.

Northwest (Maestro) was of Celt origin.

Southwest (Sirocco) was of Amazonian origin.

Southeast (Libeccio) was of Aborigine origin.

This was the last generation in the old ancestral line. It had existed for almost one thousand years. The Society knew that if it were to continue, it needed to change and adapt to the modern world.

The world had lost touch with its history. The birth of technology had transformed it beyond all recognition. People were no longer interested in rural settings. They were no longer interested in the customs and traditions of the past. They were merely interested in the future and the bright lights of the big cities.

Every Emissary was over three hundred years' old, some older than others. They were gifted with a long life. They had all been appointed at the age of thirty (the Society's age of majority).

Madame Vauqelin had cared for and taught each and every one of them from the moment they were chosen and marked with the compass until their appointment. That was her duty. Of course, she was older than any Emissary and had known three generations. She was soon to know a fourth.

The Emissaries had protected the world for centuries. They were soldiers and martyrs, like Henry.

They lived and died to protect the world. They could see into the hearts and minds of people.

Humanity could be weak and impressionable. However, more often than not, it prevailed, driven by a sense of survival and right versus wrong, it continued to fight and evolve.

Its evolution had been remarkable in the last ten years. Science and technology had leapt forward. This confused matters. Some things could not be explained by science, and technology was simply a tool. Nonetheless, their advancement had altered the thinking and expectations of people.

The world was engrossed in making money, getting rich and this purpose in life was a distraction from what was real, living and otherwise.

Computers, algorithms, artificial intelligence were shaping the world, but few truly appreciated how vulnerable the world was to being overrun by evil. Dark and powerful forces lurked deep in its shadows.

The Society was formed to resist and defeat them. Those forces had come close to overwhelming the world with the killing of Henry, but the Society had prevailed and survived. The Emissaries were tired, worn down by centuries of battle. A new generation was needed, and Tom and Zoe were to be the first.

Part 2

Stephen and Alexander

CHAPTER 10

The Rising

The curator passed down the corridor and turned into the Hall of Curiosities. It wasn't a very large space as its name inferred. Quite the opposite. It was probably only eight metres by eight metres. But curious it was indeed!

The museum filled the floors and walls of an old Regency period house on Wimpole Street. A small plaque by the door read 'Purveyors of History'. Hundreds of people walked past it every day not knowing it was there. It was just another building, just another black door. Dark red satin curtains were pulled across all the windows.

The museum didn't advertise or have a website. It was only known by those who dealt in antiquities and historical artefacts. But those who knew of it also knew what a trove of treasure it was. That was the reason for keeping its anonymity. Some of the items it housed were so precious and rare they could not be valued. That and the unquestionable fact that some could also be extremely dangerous if they were to fall in the wrong hands.

Mr. Waldly had worked at the museum for the last 50 years. Firstly, as an understudy, then as deputy curator and now as curator.

He knew every inch of the building from the squeaky floorboards to the rusting pipes. He also knew everything there was to know about its artefacts.

The Hall of Curiosities was a large open space and occupied most of the ground floor immediately beyond the reception and cloakrooms. The walls were panelled in dark mahogany and the lighting was dim.

The artefacts on display were a mix associated with religious and scientific history. They were secured in glass cases with brass trimming. The casing appeared as old and fragile as the items it protected but it was in fact extremely robust and designed to withstand a significant assault. Above each case was a brief but comprehensive description of the item together with a small map depicting its origin.

They were all unique. However, unlike the artefacts on the first floor, they were mainly ceremonial and relatively harmless.

The first floor housed the more mysterious artefacts. They were spread throughout eight rooms and organised by continent of origin: Asia, Africa, North America, South America, Europe, Australia, and Antarctica.

One could not access the first floor freely. Visits were strictly by appointment only.

The staircase leading to the first floor lay beyond a narrow door behind the reception desk. There was only enough space for one person to pass at a time. There was no other means of access.

Mr. Waldly completed his evening check of the ground floor by activating the ground floor alarm. He moved behind reception and opened the door to the first floor. He closed and locked the door behind him. The door and the wooden panelling surrounding the staircase was reinforced under the wooden panelling with steel.

The keys jangled at his waist as he slowly climbed the stairs. It was a steep climb.

Unlike the adjoining buildings which were on four low level storeys, this building was on three. The ground floor had a very high vaulted ceiling meaning that the first floor began at the level of the second floor of the adjoining building. This building had been purposefully built as a home for the museum when the terrace was constructed in 1720.

The first floor was always where the secret artefacts were stored, and it had been deliberately elevated to keep it safe from burglars. Basements were commonly used as an alternative for storage but in London they were particularly susceptible to rats and those gnawing teeth could ruin anything.

Mr. Waldly reached the top of the stairs and moved forward onto a small landing. Ahead of him was a single entrance of double doors. The ceiling was low compared to the ground floor. The doors were reinforced as with the ground floor and covered in mahogany panelling.

Mr. Waldly turned the first key to release a very large Chubb and a second to release two long and thick bolts running the length of the door.

With a single push the doors swung open to reveal the first of eight rooms. The walls were covered in green satin paper with gold inlay.

An ornate gold and crystal chandelier hung from the centre of the ceiling.

Despite the green walls, the room shimmered red.

A variety of objects sat on the floor or pedestals depending on their size. The larger objects sat on the floor.

The most immediate was what looked like a large staff. Aside from its size, it was very modest looking, crafted from wood with a spherical top. Its bottom was worn and splintered as though it had been repeatedly thrust to the ground. Behind it, propped against the wall was a shield. Again, made from wood with metal bolts spread all over its front and metallic edging.

Beyond the shield were a series of weapons - a mace, a mallet, an axe and a variety of spears both short and long.

Lying discreetly at the back of the room, a lone stone shone brightly. So brightly, it cast a shadow over everything before it. The rock sat alone in a small case on a shelf next to some very old looking texts.

Mr. Waldly surveyed the room and fixed his eyes on the stone. It flickered red in the darkness. He promptly shut the door and locked it before returning to his quarters.

CHAPTER 11

Alexander

Alexander edged slowly towards the cobbled courtyard, disturbing a flock of pigeons as he moved forward. The birds took flight all at once flapping their wings about Alexander as they climbed from the cobbles.

Alexander hunched, bent his knees, dropped to the ground and pressed his back against the stone lined archway which led into the courtyard.

As he did so, something ricocheted off the archway inches from his face and then again by his arm.

He lunged forward to the opposite side of the archway and peered down. On the cobbles lay two darts. They appeared tribal with multi-coloured feathers at the end of a very sharp wooden shaft.

Alexander needed to get to safety.

Beyond the courtyard were his halls of residence. Behind him was the library from which he had fled. It seemed hopeless trying to cross the open courtyard. Returning to the library might be the best option.

He had seen the librarian returning from her tea break and passed a large group of students entering the library as he left. Surely, whoever was after him wouldn't continue to pursue him in such a public arena?

Alexander crept out from under the archway and headed back to the library. As he moved, a third dart hit his calf.

He broke into a run but as he did so he began to feel his calf muscle tighten and his leg grow heavier. The feeling spread up his body and down to his other leg.

As he reached the door of the library, he tripped and fell, pushing himself forward as he collapsed in the entrance hall to the library.

Alexander awoke on a sofa. A chaise longue to be exact. It was designed for lounging not lying and such was the power of the poison that he barely hung from its edge.

In front of him burned an open fire. Its warmth tingled on his cheek bones.

The fireplace was surrounded by four blue tiles on each side with a simple compass design setting eight points. Various ornaments sat across the mantle but one in particular caught Alexander's eye.

A compass shone out from the mantle's centre. It was gold and sat ahead a small pole within two swivelling cylindrical circles. It was unlike anything Alexander had seen before. It was fascinating and hypnotised Alexander for at least a minute before Mrs. Jones walked into the room, closing the door sharply behind her as if to capture Alexander's attention.

"Start from the beginning," she said in a clipped and unsympathetic fashion. "Be brief now but don't leave out any details. Go!"

"Ermm, OK," Alexander stuttered.

Mrs. Jones was known at the university for her direct and punctuated speech. However, in this instance, she was being deliberately so. As a friend of the Society, she had been alerted to Alexander by them a few months ago and asked to keep an eye on him. If Alexander were in danger, so was the Society and they needed to know everything as soon as possible.

"I received a phone call last night from one of my parents' oldest friends saying he was visiting Cambridge from Russia as part of an exchange programme and wanted to meet me at the University. He is a scientist of some sort, I believe. Anyway, we agreed to meet at my halls of residence this evening. He asked me to borrow a book from the library so he could peruse it when we met. He was very specific about which one. He said there were only two copies in circulation worldwide. One in our library and the other in private ownership. A book about alchemy, 'The Compendium Of Al..'"

"'The Compendium of Alchemists' Abstruse Contrivances'," Mrs. Jones interjected.

"Yes," Alexander confirmed. "So, I set off to the library. When I arrived, I went to the desk to ask your colleague where to find it."

"Which colleague?" Mrs. Jones enquired. "I was alone yesterday. Harriet called in sick."

"A man about my height (Alexander was exceptionally tall, standing at about one hundred and ninety-five centimetres) with a shaved head."

"What time was this?" Mrs. Jones asked.

"About 6pm." Alexander replied.

Mrs. Jones paused for a second recalling her movements earlier in the day. She had gone to the kitchen around that time to make a last cup of tea, but she had only been gone for 5 minutes at most. This man must have been spying on her.

"Do carry on," she said.

"Well, I enquired where I might find the book, but he said it wasn't in the library's collection. Then he made a call on his mobile. I thought I should check the database and there it was! Aisle 6 Shelf D No. 293. So, I left the desk to find it. When I arrived at its location it wasn't there, and the same man was standing rather ominously at the far end of the aisle clutching a book. He reached into his pocket and it spooked me! I bolted for the exit as quickly as I could and left the library heading back towards my halls. I looked up and that's when I saw him in the window of my room. But that's not possible, surely? I had just left him behind at the library. He realised I had spotted him and opened the window. That's when I crouched down in the archway, but I can't remember any more."

"OK, Alexander. Stay there and rest." Miss Jones said in a rather more comforting tone. "I just need to make a phone call."

CHAPTER 12

A Call to Arms

The ringing of the phone echoed down the hallway into the main Chamber and then stopped. Next came the shuffling of feet moving swiftly along the tiled hallway floor and a soft knocking at the Chamber door.

Madam Vauqelin shouted, "Enter!", and in came Mr. Grimes, her clerk. He was a very small man indeed with a pointy nose, bushy eyebrows and a squeaky voice.

"It's Mr. Waldly from the museum for you Madame. He says it's extremely urgent."

Madame stopped her discourse, turned on her heels, and left the Chamber. The Emissaries said nothing. They sensed unrest and it was for Madame to confirm.

"Mr. Waldly, how may I help you?" she asked.

"Madame Vauqelin, it's the stone, it's awake!" Mr. Waldly exclaimed.

Madame stumbled slightly and regained her balance. Then, in a hushed tone, she said, "Mr. Waldly, please be so kind as to stay in your quarters. A Cardinal will be with you momentarily." She then replaced the handset on its cradle and returned to the Chamber.

Tramontane was already on his feet as she entered the Chamber and then, in an instant, he vanished into thin air.

Mr. Waldly heard a coded knocking at the museum door and from his window saw a very large figure looming at the entrance. He dashed downstairs and slowly opened the door.

"Good evening Mr. Waldly," the figure said "Madame has sent me to watch over the stone." And upon that the figure stepped past Mr. Waldly into the museum. The lights flickered and the air turned cold. Tramontane gave a cursory look around the ground floor.

"Is there a basement Mr. Waldly?"

"No, just the tunnel leading to Great Portland Street tube station."

"Very well, please ensure the tunnel entrance is locked and then kindly show me to the stone."

Mr. Waldly locked the main door and then moved quickly to a small hatch hidden at the back of the cloakroom. He checked it was secured and then took the visitor upstairs. Tramontane squeezed his way to the top of the staircase.

As he entered the room, he recognised the artefacts before him. They had belonged to his ancestors and had been handed down through time.

As he passed by the staff, he took it in one hand. It sparked as if electricity was passing through it and transformed into a brilliant metal. Next he took the shield which did the same.

Mr. Waldly stood discreetly in the entrance. This wasn't the first time a Emissary had visited the museum and it wouldn't be the last! Each room held mystical objects, scattered through history, lost and found, and were surrounded by the tools to protect them. The first floor was as much an armoury as it was a museum.

Tramontane took up position by the window and waited.

"You should leave Mr. Waldly, taking the tunnel would be the wisest."

"Thank you, sir, but my place is here," he replied, and he retired to his quarters.

The rain began to fall suddenly and heavily outside. So heavily that it beat against the window like a drum. Tramontane stood motionless peering onto the street below.

The street was empty as the moonlight reflected off the puddles of water collecting in the road.

Then came the sound of horses' hoofs clicking as they struck the tarmac. First faintly and then very loudly. The noise of the rainfall and hoofs was deafening. Tramontane continued to stand motionless as he watched the street below.

As quickly as the rain had started, it stopped, as did the sound of hoofs. Though he saw nothing, he could hear the horses neighing as they came to rest in front of the museum and then the distinctive sound of their passengers dismounting.

But Tramontane stayed put. Cardinals held tremendous energy but used it sparingly. Tramontane could hear them circling the building. Then, they materialised next door on both sides feeling the walls to find a weak spot. Time passed as they slid across every inch until finally, they found a way in.

The museum had been blessed many times to keep out bad

omens but nothing was impregnable.

Slowly, they slipped through appearing inside the museum as faint lines. They wafted through the air growing stronger and clearer. Tramontane could hear them outside of the room. They whispered to each other in a foreign tongue. It was as if they were chanting.

Still Tramontane stood motionless but now concentrated his gaze upon the door to the room. All at once, they entered the room.

Tramontane could barely make out their form. He slammed the staff against the floor, and it let out a blinding explosion of light. The luminescence exposed the shadows. They stood about ten feet tall.

Tramontane slammed the staff against the floor again and shouted "Burn!".

The globe at the top of the staff emitted a huge white flame which filled the room. The shadows swirled and spun, letting out a high-pitched scream. Then, they were gone. Tramontane heard the cantering of horses' hoofs in the street below and then all was quiet again.

CHAPTER 13

The Sanctuary

Tom left the school through the back gates. He had discovered from a few older boys that was the quickest way home.

However, as he walked down the street, those same boys were waiting for him on the corner.

"Come here Tom," one of the boys said in a friendly manner to lure him closer.

Tom was wary but what could he do? They were twice his size and blocking his way forward.

"Hello chaps," he said, trying to bring them on his side. He knew instinctively that something wasn't right.

"Chaps!" the biggest boy said (mocking Tom's enunciated speech), "Grab him and his bag!"

The other two hurtled forward towards Tom, who stood about twenty metres away. Tom froze, then turned and immediately bumped into Zoe.

"Hello Tom," Zoe said calmly, "Are these boys bothering you?"

"Well, sort of," Tom replied.

At that moment, the two boys reached Tom and Zoe. In one movement, Zoe stamped very hard on one of the boy's feet with her heel. A bone cracked as he fell to the floor yelping with pain.

No sooner had her heel barely touched his foot, she crouched close to the ground and exacted a thundering blow to the side of the second boy's knee. He let out a scream and collapsed.

She rose and broke into a run after the leader. He turned to escape but Zoe had already picked up a small pebble and launched it at his head. It met him squarely on the cranium and let out a small pouring of blood. His legs buckled and he rolled on the ground wincing in agony.

Then she stopped in her tracks and returned to Tom.

"Let's get you back home Tom," she said, extending her arm across Tom's back.

"Right then," Tom said as they walked past the flattened bullies.

Zoe couldn't resist kicking the leader hard in the ribs as they passed him by.

They turned the corner and headed down the hill towards the railway bridge. It was dusk and the light was fading but Tom felt safe with Zoe by his side and Zoe... well Zoe was Zoe. Nothing frightened or would deter her.

As they reached the bridge Tom noticed a large figure standing under the arches.

He pointed the figure out to Zoe.

"Hey you!" Zoe heckled, still fired up from the encounter with the bullies. "What are you doing?" she demanded.

There was no response but instead the figure emerged from the cover of the arches and began to slowly move towards Tom and Zoe.

Tom quickened his pace but Zoe held him back.

"Don't you think we've had enough confrontation for one evening? Let's keep moving," Tom pleaded. But Zoe ignored him and shouted, "What's your game then?"

All at once, the figure loomed over them and both children were hypnotised by the bright yellow eyes which peered out from under the figure's hood.

"You're quite the fighter, are you not, little girl?" the figure enquired in an ominous voice.

Zoe wanted to reply but couldn't. She couldn't part her lips, try as she might. Tom was having the same problem.

"I need you to come with me." the figure said as it reached out with both hands and held them gently across their heads.

Tom and Zoe were both trying desperately to step back but they couldn't move. It was as if they were frozen.

Then, both felt a strange sensation, a tingling in their toes, as their surroundings began to spin, first slowly and then rapidly and so much so that they both felt extremely sick.

The trees whistled in the wind and Tom realised that he could hear every noise around him. But strangely, not as one great din but individual sounds, distinct and clear as if each sound was a musician within a great orchestra playing a harmonious melody.

Tom awoke first. He looked around, taking in his setting.

The room was small but cosy. It was simply furnished with a bed on which Tom lay, a side table, small wardrobe and chair. There was no window and the walls were bare apart from a small bookshelf and a few dog-eared paperbacks.

But outside Tom could hear a bell chiming, and as he concentrated, he heard chatter.

"We must protect him at all costs!" the voices murmured. "And the girl. Do you realise who they are and what they can achieve together? They are us. I mean the new us. A better us. An 'us' fit for this new world."

Where is Zoe? Tom suddenly thought. They were together under the bridge. What happened? Tom's memory was failing him. They left school together. Zoe beat up the bullies. They were walking home under the bridge and then... Tom just couldn't recall. A complete blank.

At that moment, Tom heard a knock at the door and keys turning in the lock. The door handle turned, and the door opened slowly.

Madam Vauqelin appeared in the doorway.

"Hello, my dear," she said with a soothing voice. "How are you feeling?"

"A little sore," Tom replied. "And thirsty."

"I'll fetch you something to drink," Madam Vauqulin said. "You need to rest."

"Where am I?" Tom asked.

"Somewhere safe." Madam Vauqelin replied. And with that she left the room. This time she left the door ajar.

Tom peered around the door out onto a very long cloistered walkway; so long in fact that Tom struggled to see the end clearly. The other side of the path was made up of a long line of open arches which gave onto what appeared to be an ornamental garden.

It was daytime and the sun was shining brightly, quite a contrast to the gloomy wet night before. The air smelled different as well, fresher. Not the usual heavy smoke-filled city air.

Tom stepped out of the room and was immediately greeted by a cat. She was a grey tortoiseshell with yellow eyes. The cat wove in and out of Tom's legs rubbing herself against his feet and then rolled back and forth on her back, craving attention. Tom bent down and rubbed her tummy. He suddenly recognised his cat.

"Lucy?" he said.

She let out a long rumbling purr.

"I see you've found Lucy," Madame Vauqelin said.

Tom looked up and saw Madame holding a tray. He rose to his feet and offered to take the tray. Madame Vauqelin declined and suggested he find a place in the garden to settle and enjoy the refreshments.

They walked down some stone steps onto a gravelled path. The garden was in the form of a hexagon surrounded by an outer path and dissected by eight paths which met at the garden's centre.

"Let's sit in the middle," Tom suggested.

"Very good." Madame replied.

They both walked side by side towards the centre and Lucy ran ahead.

"Where am I and how did I come to be here? How did Lucy come to be here?" Tom enquired.

"You're in our sanctuary Tom. One of the Emissaries brought you here with Zoe"

"Where is Zoe?"

"She's still resting Tom. You woke first."

"My parents will be worried sick. I need to call them."

"They have been contacted, Tom. You're here with their blessing."

With that, they reached the centre of the garden. A beautiful wooden pagoda filled the space and around it grew roses of every colour and variety.

"They're my hobby. Very difficult to grow properly you know. I've created a few species of my own over the years." Madame said.

Tom looked at Madame pondering her age. She seemed to be in her seventies but was very sprightly.

Tom felt very relaxed. His anxiety had left him and been replaced by a feeling of serenity. He was very much at ease and comfortable with his surroundings as if he were at home with his parents.

Madame and Tom talked at length. Tom wanted to understand where he was exactly and why he had been brought there. Madame explained that Tom was special and that his path in life had been prescribed from birth.

She always found these initial conversations with Emissaries very difficult. She never wanted to divulge too much information so as to frighten but equally wanted to explain enough to inform and educate. It was especially difficult with Tom. He was the youngest Emissary in history and remarkably inquisitive.

As the conversation deepened, Tom felt a yearning. He was very confident but there had always been an element of uncertainty. Something was missing. Something he knew would make him complete.

Tom looked at Madame and asked, "Who am I? I mean who am I really? You know, don't you? You can tell me everything. Can't you?"

Madame smiled and replied, "All in good time Tom but let's just say you're someone special."

"Tom! Tom!"

Tom looked up and saw Zoe running down the path towards him.

"I'm so happy to see you!" She exclaimed as she reached him. And with that she grabbed his arm, pulled him up and hugged him so tightly that it hurt.

Behind Zoe stood a very tall figure. Tom immediately recognised its yellow eyes. The figure was hooded, and Tom remembered it from the night before.

"That's Maestro, Zoe said."

Maestro removed her hood revealing her face. She had long jet black hair and a very pale complexion; almost pure white.

"Maestro brought us here last night Tom."

Madame made a discrete gesture with her hand and Maestro nodded, replacing her hood and returned down the path towards the building.

Tom and Zoe looked at each other and smiled. Something between them felt right. They were almost jubilant together despite recent events.

CHAPTER 14

Dobro Pozhalovat

Alexander was an Oxford undergraduate of History.

He was the only child of Mr. and Mrs. Turgenev from St. Petersburg, Russia. They were both successful businesspeople. His father ran a jewelry company and his mother ran an art gallery.

Alexander had been named after his father's favourite poet - Alexander Pushkin.

His family had been part of the Russian nobility before the Bolshevik revolution but its roots could be traced back to the Mongol Empire.

Alexander woke from his slumber. The clock on the mantlepiece was chiming. It was midnight. He had been sleeping for at least an hour. Alexander rubbed his eyes and sat up.

There was a knock at the door and Mrs. Jones entered. Behind her appeared a man so tall and wide that he made everything around him seem infinitesimally small. He ducked, almost to a right angle, just to make it through the doorway.

"This is Ostro," Mrs. Jones explained, "He's going to look after you, Alexander. Do, as he asks, please." And with that, Mrs. Jones left the room.

"I'm pleased to meet you Alexander," Ostro said in a deep rumbling tone. "We need to get going so if you will?" Ostro swung his cloak. The room spun and Alexander felt everything around him fall away. He tried desperately to stay conscious for as long as possible.

The sensation of teleportation was too much to bear for most people. Only those who practised it were used to its effects. Even the Emissaries only resorted to it in times of emergency. It put a huge strain on the body and mind.

Alexander saw nothing around him but bright strips of light of every colour and he felt the tight grip of Ostro's hand around his arm. Then, all at once, everything ground to a halt with one short sharp jolt. Alexander was standing (or rather staggering) in a small room furnished with a bed and wardrobe.

He turned to Ostro to speak but before he could say a word he vomited and collapsed into his arms.

Alexander awoke a few hours later. His evening had been a very strange and stressful one and he was convinced that he had been dreaming.

He reached over to where he thought his alarm clock would be only to find a blank space. As his eyes opened wider and his vision cleared, he realised that he was not in his room at university but somewhere else. Ahead of him was a wardrobe and chair. He lifted himself up and opened the door and peered out onto the very same gardens in which Tom, Zoe and Madame were sitting.

He wandered out and followed the sound of their voices. As he approached them, Madame called out to him,

"Alexander, you're awake already. We were sure you'd be sleeping for a few hours still. Ostro told me you had remained conscious during the journey. Quite remarkable you know? It's never happened before. People usually pass out. You're a tough cookie my dear."

Zoe fidgeted in her seat such was her competitive nature. She didn't like to be beaten at anything and that was how she saw it. As for being 'tough', that was a title she wanted all for herself. It wasn't to be shared with anyone in her mind - boy or not.

"Where am I?" Alexander asked.

"Well," Madame said, "I was just coming onto that. Please take a seat Alexander. There are some refreshments here if I can tempt you."

Then Madame began to tell them about the Society.

"We are known as the Society and our members called 'Emissaries' are from lands running across the eight points of the globe.

The Society was founded in the late part of the eleventh century by the Master Navigators. In the beginning, they were explorers.

Their aim was to collect artefacts from around the world in order to preserve cultures and history which were being plundered by the unscrupulous colonialists and pirates. They acquired many treasures from their travels and learnt things about the world which most never knew existed.

In time, they became very powerful people. But they swore an oath - *'Bene Facitis Et Defendat'*. Literally, it translated as *'Do Good And Defend'*.

They became experts in the mystical arts practised across the continents. They discovered how to manipulate the elements and see through dimensional planes. And lastly, they learnt the art of teleportation which is how you were all brought here."

Tom, Zoe and Alexander listened in silence quite perplexed by what they were hearing. Was this true? Could it be believed? Surely, this was fantasy. It couldn't be possible, teleportation!

Madame was used to such reactions. She had recounted the story so many times to the current and past Emissaries and it always elicited the same response - sheer disbelief. But they would learn and come to understand soon enough. In fact, they would have to, for the survival of humanity

Madame said, "My dears, let's go inside, I would like to introduce you to the Emissaries."

Madame, Tom, Zoe and Alexander walked back down the path and Lucy skipped ahead.

CHAPTER 15

Stephen

Stephen was with his friends travelling on the 17:35 train from Waterloo.

They were all trainee lawyers who worked at firms around the city.

Stephen was born and had been raised by his mother in London. His parents had separated when he was only three years' old.

He had an IQ of one hundred and eighty and obtained a first-class degree in Law from Cambridge at the age of nineteen.

He had just turned twenty and had been left unconvinced by his experiences thus far in the Law. He had been contemplating a change in career but had little idea what would make a good alternative for him. Fate would decide for him.

Looking at these young trainees, one would not believe that they assisted in advising some of the biggest corporate clients in town. They still acted like teenagers. They had no awareness of the space and people around them.

They each had a four pack of beer, crisps and a mascot bear and brought life to an otherwise dull carriage with their chatter and laughter.

The train was headed to the south coast where Stephen and his friends were joining others for a weekend of festivity and fun.

Stephen was a very sociable lad and always up for an adventure wherever it took him. This weekend he wasn't going to be disappointed. He would soon be joining Tom, Zoe and Alexander.

The train rocked from side to side as it travelled along the track. Stephen and his friends chatted amongst themselves exchanging anecdotes about their colleagues and offices. The sky grew darker.

Stephen felt tired. It had been a long day. It had started with a breakfast meeting at 8am followed by a marathon conference call with the New York and Paris office which finished just before 4pm. He hadn't been able to stop for lunch and ran out of the office at 5pm to make it to the station on time. The rush had caught up with him now and he dozed off to the amusement of his friends.

He awoke what seemed moments later. Something felt very odd. He looked around and realised that his friends were gone. To the bar he thought.

He looked up and down the carriage and realised that it was empty. Not a soul in sight. Not a sound. He looked outside and could barely make out his surroundings. The sky was the darkest of greys, almost black and he realised that the train had come to a standstill.

He stood up and moved warily down the carriage. As he advanced towards the doors, he realised they were wooden. In fact, the whole carriage had a wooden frame and was unrecognisable to the carriage he had sat in with his friends at the start of the journey.

Gas burners glowed on each side and the windows were draped with green velour curtains. Where was he? Surely this was an elaborate practical joke, he thought.

He arrived at the door and reached out to the brass handle, but, before he touched it, the door slid open abruptly. He reached for his stomach as he crouched forward in pain from severe cramp. Sharp pangs drove him back as he felt people walking through his body. Voices swirled around him, but he could not make out what they were saying. He stood up and looked about him but saw nothing. He continued to hear voices and children crying.

He stepped out of the carriage and turned towards the exit. A face appeared at the window. It was pale and sickly with blood shot bespectacled eyes. It gave him a melancholic regard then disappeared.

Stephen felt wretched. Worse than he had ever felt before. He needed some fresh air. Looking more closely out of the window he realised that the train was on a platform. He turned the handle and stepped down. The air was filled with heavy smoke.

Stephen moved cautiously down the platform. It was dimly lit with more gas lamps hanging from posts. Ahead of him was a building and no doubt the ticket office he thought but the windows were darkened, and it didn't seem as if anyone was inside.

Then he heard a short whistle as the train began to pull away from the platform. Stephen turned swiftly and tried to reopen the train door, but it wouldn't open. He ran beside the train to the end of the platform and then watched it disappear into the fog.

He felt like someone was watching him from the building and once again he advanced carefully towards it. As he drew closer, he caught the fluttering of a shadow at the window. Someone or something was inside. On the door was a tired sign which simply read 'OPEN'. Stephen duly obliged as the door creaked on its hinges.

He entered a brightly lit room full of people - adults and children. They all turned sharply and looked at him intensely. They were dressed in antiquated clothing, and all had a very pale complexion and bloodshot eyes.

Stephen felt very unwelcome indeed and quickly reversed out of the doorway shutting the door in front of him. He stood there momentarily. Then, Stephen opened the door again.

This time the room was empty and dark. There was no one in sight and Stephen choked on the dust and acrid smell floating around the room. Stephen edged cautiously into the room and as he cleared the doorway the door slammed shut behind him.

He stood motionless for a few seconds and then started to hear whispering and sniggering. The voices grew louder until he could eventually make out the words.

"He doesn't belong. He's strange. Get rid of him!"

"Cut him, maim him, kill him!", they were saying.

Stephen panicked. He reached for the door and tugged at it but it wouldn't budge. He felt a scratching at his back which became more and more intense. He turned to fight back but tripped and fell to the floor.

At that moment, the door opened slightly, and a hand reached in. "Take it", a voice said. He obeyed and was dragged out of the room. He heard shrieking back in the room and glanced to see the bloodshot eyes peering angrily at him as he was pulled to safety.

"We mustn't linger. It's extremely dangerous here", the large looming figure beside him spoke in a hushed tone. "This is the last stop on the line. A place where all things living end. How did you find yourself here young man?"

"I have no idea", Stephen replied, as he rose to his feet. He was still in shock and his back was throbbing with the pain of the clawing.

"I must deliver you to Madame without delay. You will need her powers of healing".

The figure lifted his cloak and enveloped Stephen as he fell into a stupor and passed out.

CHAPTER 16

The Wiccan

She sat cross-legged on the Heath.

The dawn sun was rising, and moisture rose from the grass around her creating an ever-thickening mist.

She sat at the exact point the ley lines crossed from north to south running across the earth. This was a powerful position both for light and dark.

Her eyes were firmly shut as her mind filled with images.

She had seen Stephen on the train as it pulled into the platform, but she could no longer see him or the figure who had saved him from certain death at the railway station.

Yet, she knew where they were travelling. Stephen would soon be at the Sanctuary and that was what the Wiccan wished to visualise. Its location was the greatest secret of all. The home of the Society of Eight.

Only Society members knew of its existence but that was about to change. The Wiccan had been working on her plan for two hundred and fifty years and the time had come to strike during the Emissaries' transition.

She began to rock from left to right, then forwards and backwards all the while remaining silent. Then she stopped and her head shuddered violently. She opened her eyes and let out a sharp cry and then smiled.

She could see the heart of the Sanctuary - the great Chamber. The place where all eight Emissaries sat. And on the floor, the windrose. She projected herself and stood at its center taking in everything around her.

Of course, this was only in her mind's eye but very soon she would be there in person and bring its hallowed walls tumbling down, decimating everything around it, until the Sanctuary, the centuries' old home of this ancient society, was no more. Gone forever.

CHAPTER 17

The Cimmerian

Deep beneath the city, amongst the caverns and relics of times gone by there existed a room. In this room, sat three pedestals and on each pedestal stood a statue. The statues were all very different.

The first was in the form of a beautiful female figure dressed in a flowing robe. Her hair twisted and turned around her body, and on her chest, she wore an amulet. Within the amulet was laid a magnificent white pearl. Her eyes seemed to shimmer with light even though they were made of stone.

The second was difficult to make out. It was contorted and warped. An animal or monster of some kind. Long curling claws gripped the pedestal on all four corners. Its head lay on the pedestal between the front feet looking up. Its eyes were asymmetric and bulbous, and a large hooked beak protruded from its mouth. Its scaled body rose about eight feet into the air and was topped by an even longer tail which wove itself this way and that around the beast and back down to the pedestal.

The third was a young child. By appearances, a boy. He held a basket which was spilling over with what seemed, on first glance, fruit or food of some sort. On closer inspection, it was in fact small serpents and insects.

A circle was carved into the floor running around the statues as were lines which ran between the statues to make a triangle. At the center of the triangle was an eye and around it within the circle were scattered a myriad of symbols both new and old. Hieroglyphic, Cyrillique, Ancient Greek and Latin were amongst them. But also, stranger symbols using crudely drawn figures of grotesque creatures.

Beyond the statues lay three steep and wide steps rising into the wall behind them. Above the top step was a carving of a goat's head. On its brow was an odd symbol made up of a double cross standing on top of the infinity sign (figure '8' on its side).

A constant sound circled the room. It was shrill but low as if it were muffled. It ran through every bit of stone in the room and bounced around as if it were desperate to escape. It pounded the floor and the walls. Then it smashed against the ceiling and returned to the floor again. Around and around it span until it climbed piercing the ceiling and searing higher and higher through the foundations above it until it emerged into the night air shrieking and screaming as it climbed into the sky.

The lights of the East End riverside shone brightly below. It was summer and the streets were full with the hustle and bustle of the night markets. A parade of stalls ran along the water edge. Some people heard the shrill sound as it climbed above them looking up to see what it was.

Eventually, it stopped climbing and began to fall much faster than it rose. As it fell the sound became audibly louder. The people in the market began to stop their business and look up. The sky was dark but clear. The people peered but could not see anything. The sound became deafening as it approached the market.

The Thames water had been lying still but now began to ripple and splash hard against the quay. Anything made of glass in the market shattered. The beast plunged into the water and entered an aqueduct which eventually gave onto a tunnel.

The Cimmerian advanced at lightning speed. Greek mythology described it as the dead locked in perpetual mist and darkness. It was an apt description. It was destined to roam the world for eternity and spread death in its wake. To end the world. At this moment, it was focussed on the Sanctuary.

CHAPTER 18

The Passing

A network of subterranean tunnels ran across the globe converging on the Sanctuary and if one knew which route to take a journey could take minutes rather than days.

The tunnels were known only to the Society and its most trusted emissaries but the Wiccan, in the guise of a peddler, had made sure all those years ago in Calicut that Captain Richard Maynard would pass the Red Lodestone to the Society and thereafter it would only be a matter of time before she located the Sanctuary. It had taken a little over 250 years, but the time had finally come.

The captain was oblivious to the witch's trickery and by the time he was brought into the Sanctuary as an emissary himself he was under her spell. Such was the power of the enchantment that neither the Emissaries nor Madame herself had the faintest notion.

It had been predicted in the Society's annals that the stone would be delivered to them by a master mariner and that it would bring the Society great power and protection. Thus, it had been accepted willingly by the Society and installed within its home. In this respect, it was unique as all the other artefacts upon which the Society relied were hidden in key locations across the globe.

Alas, the Red Lodestone would lead to the very destruction of the Society's home.

The group were led into the Chamber and asked to take their respective cathedra (ceremonial chair). Tom was directed by Emissary Tramontane to the North chair. Zoe was directed to the Northwest chair by Emissary Maestro. Alexander was directed to the Northeast chair by Emissary Grecale. Finally, Stephen was directed to the South chair by Emissary Ostro.

The compass was incomplete but there was no time to waste. For the sake of the group and the future of the Society, the transition had to be made immediately.

The four Emissaries stood behind the group in their place as Madame Vauqelin entered the Chamber. There was another bang in the sky and tremors below.

All at once the group felt a shudder which shattered their inner core. They slumped forward like dolls and lay motionless for a second. Then they rose as quickly as they had fallen. Their eyes were wide, shining yellow. Their Emissaries stood behind them with eyes shining yellow also.

The transition was happening but not as anticipated. Four of the new generation and four Emissaries were missing. Their power was severely diminished. But it was all they had.

The great stone carvings on the wall began to crumble and slip away from the walls and the glass dome began to shake.

The Emissaries surrounded the group and tried to transport them but couldn't. Madame Vauqelin ran towards the ornate metal doors. She had to reach the key.

A rose gold ball was set in the centre of the left door. Around it lay several icons. Twisting and turning the ball in the right order and pushing the ball would open two hidden entrances leading to tunnels outside of the Sanctuary.

The combination was complicated. Madame had set it herself but, in this chaos, struggled to recall it. She turned the ball one way and another. All the while the tremors grew, and she knew it would just be a few minutes before the Cimmerian crashed through the floor of the Sanctuary.

Madame made one last twist of the ball and then pushed it as hard as she could into the door. All at once, the doors began to tick and clang as the locks buried within its iron panels opened one after the other.

Several seconds passed before one final clang released huge springs either side of the main doors. As they plunged forward, the stone slabs surrounding the doors shifted to reveal two tunnels beyond them.

"Tom and Zoe take the left tunnel and Alexander and Stephen take the right tunnel. Go now!" She yelled.

The Emissaries grabbed their protégées and led them into the tunnels. Once they were clear Madame pulled a lever beneath the ball and the stone slabs slowly shifted back into place sealing the tunnels. Tom glanced back towards the entrance and saw Madame smiling at him as the Cimmerian beyond her smashed through the Chamber floor. The entrance sealed shut.

Madame drew a deep breath as the beast rose above her climbing towards the glass dome. She shifted her bright orange cape to one side and lifted her staff skyward.

Madame Vauqelin was the Warden of the Emissaries. They were her children, and this was their home. It was too late to save. That Madame knew. But she would never allow its secrets to be taken. She waited for the beast to reach the dome and shouted

"Vur Ha!" as she slammed her staff into the ground. It was the Society's war cry and literally meant "Strike!".

As the Cimmerian smashed through the dome everything around it slowed to a virtual standstill. A blinding light shone through the sky turning it to a brilliant turquoise. The shattered glass hung in the air. The compass at the top of the dome was suspended in the air spinning furiously until Madame whispered. "Donus." It dove into Madame's hand at lightning speed.

She felt a presence behind her and turned to find the Wiccan floating above the abyss staring at Madame through her black lifeless eyes.

The Wiccan was caught within Madame's command. She had emerged just at the point the staff struck the ground. The Wiccan was powerful and had dreamt of this moment for centuries. The Cimmerian lay paralysed in the sky above her.

The Wiccan was determined to break free.

She summoned all her force and managed to blink; first once then twice and a third time. Madame knew her command would not hold her forever, but this was too soon. Her face began to twitch lightly then more heavily. Then she raised her head up and down but all the time keeping her stare on Madame. Madame heard a loud crack as the Wiccan moved her left arm.

That was all the Wiccan needed. She lifted her arm slowly and opened her hand. Her long and skeletal fingers stretched wide.

Smoke and darkness began to fill the Sanctuary. Madame knew it was lost.

The Wiccan lifted her thin lips to break into a gradual and sinister smile as her tall skinny frame floated toward Madame. Her straight white hair fluttered in the vacuum she had created behind her.

Madame lifted her staff to strike the floor and halt the Wiccan but was too slow. Madame felt the Wiccan's overwhelming force lift her from the Chamber floor until both were centimetres from each other. The Wiccan reached into her pocket from which she drew a blade.

It was no ordinary blade. It was of course enchanted but more importantly cursed. The blade was ancient, centuries older than the Wiccan and Madame. It was made of bone with jagged edges. On its face was painted a multitude of birds (or more accurately crows) to represent death.

Madame closed her eyes. She had not foreseen this moment. It was not written in the scrolls, but it was about to happen. She summoned all the will and strength she could as her staff began to glow.

The Wiccan grabbed Madame and ran her fingers across her brow savouring every moment. She drew her arm as far behind her as she could. She waited to see if Madame would open her eyes, but they were kept firmly shut.

The Wiccan's smile faded slowly replaced by a sullen look of steely resolve. Then in one single and swift motion she brought her arm forward and plunged the blade into the heart of Madame. Madame threw her head back, her eyes opened wide and her pupils dilated as she stared upward to the circling Cimmerian.

A flock of hundreds of crows filled the Chamber. Their crowing was deafening. It muffled the last breath of Madame as her pupils shrunk, her eyes closed and she fell into the abyss below.

The Wiccan's regard followed Madame's body until it could be seen no more for the darkness. Then, she rose towards the Cimmerian which in turn engulfed her in a swirl.

The first phase of Wiccan's plan was complete. The Sanctuary had been routed. Its very soul had been torn asunder. Its Warden had been vanquished and the Emissaries were little more than fugitives.

Soon, she thought, all humanity would be entirely at her mercy. But first, she must gather an army. In an instant, the Cimmerian and the Wiccan had vanished.

Part 3

Charlotte

CHAPTER 19

Charlotte

The sea air permeated into the nearby town. It was so refreshing, relaxing and above all reinvigorating.

Charlie ran through the town centre searching for the treasure. It was the town's treasure hunt day and she was, as ever, determined to win it.

Each contestant had started from a boat moored 1km out at sea and swam against the tide to shore. From there, they ran following a series of clues up the cliffs and into the town centre. Charlie was the clear leader as she darted across the cobbled streets.

She was born and raised in Dorset. She loved the coast, the sea and above all freedom. Yet, like Zoe, also loved a game and competing.

Charlie was a tall girl. She stood at 5 feet and eleven inches. Her frame was like that of an athlete. Her shoulders were broad and square. Her waistline was narrow, and her legs were long and muscular. Her dark blonde hair was woven with streaks of gold having been bleached by the coastal sunshine. It had always been slightly tangled. Charlie was a naturally beautiful girl, but she had never been much fussed about aesthetics and appearance.

The crowds cheered as she advanced towards the finishing line. She had won the race for every age category since fifteen. Try as they might, people travelled from all over to beat her, but nobody had come close.

Suddenly, she felt a hand on her shoulder as if someone were dragging her backwards. She slowed her pace and turned but saw nothing. She felt it again. Her skin broke out in goosebumps. Then someone or something pulled at her hair but there was no one near her.

The sound of the crowd faded until it was a distant cry, but the people were right next to her. How could that be?

She felt a short, sharp jolt and found herself staring at an old shopping arcade. She didn't recognise it. The entrance was made up of three cast iron archways. One large flanked by two smaller. Above the archways was a semi-circle window and above that was a small, curved stone balcony which was topped by a very ornate gold leaf clock set over red brick. Either side of the clock were two red brick turrets.

Charlie stood in front of the gated archways and was drawn by a pale figure looking down at her from the window above. She did not know but it was the same pale figure Stephen had encountered at the station.

The figure's eyes were bloodshot and as far as she could make out it was dressed in an old black suit and white shirt. It lifted its hand and extended a finger pointing directly at Charlie. Charlie was transfixed. Everything around her was clouded. She could just make out the crowds but heard nothing but a low-pitched din.

She turned back towards the arcade. The figure was now directly in front of her behind the closed gate, its finger still pointed at her.

Aside from the eyes, there was something very strange and inhuman about the figure. Its body was dangly, and its gait was twisted as if its joints were dislocated.

Despite this rather disturbing presence, Charlie moved forward and turned the large ringed handle to open the gate. The figure slowly stepped back and turned to walk into the arcade as Charlie pushed open the gate.

The gate screeched and Charlie found herself inside the arcade as the figure disappeared inside the building.

Dust filled the air together with the musty smell of rotting wood. Broken tiles were strewn across the ground which made a crunching sound as Charlie moved forward. The arcade was on two floors.

Either side of the arcade were empty units. Each unit had a dark wooden facade with rolling window frames. The windows were so dirty that Charlie could not see inside.

Charlie kept moving forward until she reached a green marble fountain. It looked like it had long since stopped working. She touched the fountain and was alarmed when a jet of water spurted out of its centre.

At the same time, she started to hear whispering from the gallery above as apparitions of people walking along it took shape.

Her eyes wandered downward and she was baffled to see the arcade lit and busy with shoppers. The people's clothes looked Victorian.

The floor was undamaged shining bright with multicoloured tiles and the shop windows were clean and filled with goods.

There were milliners, haberdashers, tailors, cobblers, tanners, butchers, bakers, grocers, barbers, pharmacists, newsagents, confectioners, chocolatiers amongst many others.

A quartet of violinists was playing on the concourse and children ran along it, giggling and carrying balloons. Charlie watched them and smiled nervously. She had to pinch herself because none of this had existed moments earlier.

Suddenly, Charlie felt a searing pain rip through her body as an elderly woman literally passed straight through her. The woman was walking a small terrier dog. The dog stopped and stared up at Charlie and growled. Then it started barking furiously at her. The woman pulled at its lead and had not seemed to have noticed Charlie but then, out of the blue, stared straight into Charlie's eyes.

"You don't belong here!" the woman shouted. "Get away!"

Charlie was rocked by the ferocity of the woman's words. She was very disoriented and clutched first at her stomach and then at her head. What or where on earth was this place?

Suddenly, she noticed everyone in the arcade had stopped what they were doing and were peering at her. Slowly, a crowd formed around her and began to jeer.

"Get away, get away! You don't belong! Leave this place!"

Charlie turned to make her way to the gates, but they were gone. In their place was a dark brown brick wall covered in posters and advertisements.

The crowd was closing in on her forcing her back towards the wall. As they drew closer, she realised that their skin was very pale, and their eyes had turned blood-shot just like the figure which had enticed her into the arcade.

She looked high and low for an exit.

To her left, adjacent to the wall, was what looked like an antiques shop. Its window was filled with trinkets of every shape and variety. At its centre was a clock. It began to chime quietly and then more loudly. Charlie was transfixed by its tone.

She walked briskly towards the shop and noticed that the crowd would not follow her. Then she broke into a run up until the shop door. As she reached for the brass handle to open the door, the blind covering the glass door panel snapped up to reveal the face of Mr. Waldly.

He opened the door hurriedly and said,

"How did you come to be here? Come in quickly my dear. It's very unsafe out there."

Naturally, Charlie obliged and Mr. Waldly quickly closed the door and blind behind her.

"I need to call somebody", he said.

"Wait here and do not go near that door!"

"Who are those people? What are they?" Charlie enquired.

"They are the Unremembered," Mr. Waldly replied. "Forgotten and tormented souls if you will. Now I must make a call!"

With that, Mr. Waldly dashed to the back of the shop.

Mr. Waldly came from a long line of Custodians and curators of artefacts to the Society. He had been involved in many paranormal incidents.

Since the incident at the museum in London, Mr. Waldly had been tasked with finding any artefacts which had become active. Not all artefacts existed in our reality. Some existed on other plains such as that of the Unremembered.

Mr. Waldly collected and managed those artefacts at his shops and the museum.

He could travel from one plane to the next by stepping through the right door at the right time whereupon he was mostly able to disguise himself as an inhabitant.

Mr. Waldly's always wore the same attire come rain or shine: a black trilby with black satin band; a black heavy cotton overcoat; a brown wool single breasted suit with peak lapels, matching waistcoat and pleated turn-up trousers; white shirt; brown tie and black leather brogues.

His shoes were always polished to a bright shine, his clothes pressed, and tie-knot pushed tight against his shirt collars. He was ex-military having served 10 tours in the Queen's Regiment and awarded the Victoria Cross for his valour and bravery.

On his wrist, Mr. Waldly wore his treasured watch, a 1937 Charles Nicholas Tramelan Chronograph with Roman numerals. Its movement was the most reliable Landeron Calibre 51 and the watch was a rare edition whose mechanism incorporated a compass. Its case was triple nickel plated with a stainless-steel back, its face cover was reinforced, and the strap was made of brown kangaroo leather. Reputedly, the strongest leather of all.

Every Custodian chose a watch at the beginning of their service. Of course, the watches were bespoke and came with the necessary alterations to fulfil their special purpose. With it, he knew exactly when to pass through the right door.

Mr Waldly picked up the phone. It was a GPO 746 Rotary. He dialled 8421. It rang and rang but there was no answer. This was unheard of. Mr. Waldly shivered. Where was Madame?

"Charlie!", he heckled from the back of the shop. "Hurry, follow me!".

She flew from the shop front, leaving the peering eyes of the Unremembered behind her, and joined Mr. Waldly.

"Not a moment to lose, he exclaimed."

He looked at his watch. Tick tock, tick tock. The Unremembered were pushing against the shop windows and turning at the door handle. Tick tock, tick tock. A window cracked under the pressure and the wood of the door split as it opened.

All at once, the clocks in the shop chimed and Mr. Waldly grabbed Charlie's hand and thrust open the door in front of him.

He yanked her through as they appeared in a space which very much resembled a broom cupboard. It smelt of bleach, dust and stale water.

Mr. Waldly promptly shut the door behind him and opened the next door. He led Charlie into a shop. She looked around to see tinned food, toiletries, a fridge full of soft and alcoholic beverages which ran onto newspapers. This looked like a convenience store, she thought.

They passed through the shop quickly. As they reached the exit, someone said, "Mr. Waldly you can't leave my shop without buying something. You know that!"

Mr. Waldly stopped and turned to the voice.

"I'm terribly sorry Mr. Singh. We are in an awful rush."

"All the same," said Mr. Singh, the shop owner, "Dues are dues!".

With that, Mr. Waldly grabbed a packet of raspberry bonbons and several chewy nougat caramel and chocolate brownie bars. He reached into his pocket and drew a £10 note leaving it on the counter.

"Thank you again and keep the change Mr. Singh," he said as he pulled Charlie out of the shop into the cold night. It was going to be a long journey.

CHAPTER 20

The Wretched

They snivelled and stank. They lived in the sewers and knew nothing other than bad deeds. They were vile and pests on the world. They were abundant and deprived.

These creatures had survived by the generosity and naivety of others. These weasels were pure villainous scum. They preyed on the goodwill of honest hardworking people.

Their leader Graken (or "the Grand Master" as he liked to call himself) was huge and obese. He stood at about seven feet. He spluttered when he spoke owing to his missing front teeth. His belly hung out over his trousers. His eyes were deeply set and tiny compared to his balloon shaven head.

On each side of him sat his henchmen. To the right, sat Scroat and to the left, sat Krale.

Scroat was male (if one could ever tell the difference between the Wretched genders). He stood at about 5 feet 10 inches. He wore very tight trousers which were too short and exaggerated his disproportionately large posterior. His slippers were hole ridden and his socks were odd. His hair was receding and patchy through which one could see red infected boils oozing white puss. On his head, he wore oversized bulbous goggles. His teeth were rotten like all Wretched.

Krale was female. She was very short and round with plump little spotty legs. She believed she was a belle but like all other

Wretched she was a disgusting picture of dirt, sweat and infection. She combed her short black thin hair with her filthy fingers and had a strange squint in her right eye which became more pronounced as she grew anxious.

Scroat and Krale squirmed beside Graken. They giggled and writhed in the mud-laden ground.

Below Graken sat Crag his pet dog. Crag was a cross Doberman, Rottweiler and Pitbull. He was one big lump of muscle with legs and little else. To say this dog was stupid was a major understatement. Crag knew only how to eat, sleep, excrete and fight.

These diseased creatures were truly the most depraved and lascivious beings. They were driven by greed. They were corrupt and duplicitous beyond redemption. It was for this reason they were forsaken by all humanity and in return they hated humanity.

"I am told we need to act", spluttered Graken.

"Move!" he shouted.

Scroat and Krale leapt to their feet (as fast as the Wretched could move which was very slow owing to their sickly demeanour) and hobbled to the large wooden door. The door gave onto a mountainside and beyond that a large valley.

Scroat opened the door and blew on a bugle he carried on his belt.

All at once, the valley ground began to move as the Wretched emerged from their underground caverns by the thousands and then tens of thousands and then hundreds of thousands. A huge army amassed, all carrying crudely fashioned weapons of all shapes and sizes.

CHAPTER 21

The Great Cats

These magnificent beasts lived in small communes around the globe.

They were hidden from sight and possessed the power to camouflage themselves as they moved amongst the world.

They were always born of their species once a century as twins - sister and brother. The lions, the tigers, the leopards, the pumas, the jaguars, the cheetahs, the lynx, the ocelots, the caracals, the margays and last but certainly not least felis libica libica - the African wildcats.

However, the Great Cats were bigger and faster than their ordinary counterparts and above all magical. They shared a long history with the Society and had always been at their side in times of trouble. They were linked psychically to the Emissaries and tracked them during their journeys to ensure their safety. They were never far away.

Some of the cats were near the Sanctuary when it was attacked.

They knew there was little that they could do when faced with such power. All they could do was be present and to hand if the Emissaries needed them.

They paced back and forth impatient and distressed and growling in their own separate fashions. However, when the dome fell, they stopped pacing and stood motionless, stunned into silence by what they were witnessing.

The pack was led by the puma. She was the oldest and had served all the Emissaries. Her name was Shena. She could feel a great loss. She knew the worst had befallen Madame and there was nothing to be done. She bowed her head and rubbed the side of her face across the ground and pined. The other cats followed suit.

This land was holy to them. They had stood by the Sanctuary and walked within it for ions, but it had been desecrated and crumbled before them.

Their pining grew until all at once they let out an almighty roar which echoed for miles around. Then, they sloped across the debris to the precipice and one by one disappeared into the deep abyss in search of Madame's body.

CHAPTER 22

Green

Emissary Tramontane emerged from the tunnel first. He waved his hand and the huge tentacle-like roots of an old oak tree parted slowly to reveal the opening above him.

He climbed out and surveyed the surrounding woodland moving forward cautiously.

It was autumn and piles of leaves lay on the ground in every direction.

Tramontane held up his hand once more and swivelled 360 degrees as a strong gust blew the leaves away clearing the land around him. Then, he beckoned to Tom and Zoe and Maestro who emerged. Maestro remained at the rear guarding the Tom and Zoe from behind.

"The château is not far," Tramontane said. "Perhaps a day's trek around the lake and up into the mountain over there." Tramontane pointed across a wide-open lake to the East.

"Let's get on with it then." Zoe exclaimed full of her usual zeal.

"No, we will rest a while." Maestro retorted. "You have been through a great deal these last few hours. You need to recover your strength for what lies ahead."

Maestro pulled a bag from her cloak pocket and a gourde. In the bag were three bread rolls. She gave one each to Tom and Zoe and shared the third with Tramontane. Tom and Zoe scoffed the rolls in a second. They were famished. Maestro and Tramontane smiled and handed their halves to the children to finish.

Tom was exhausted. He looked out onto the lake.

The sky was overcast but a ray of sunshine cut through the clouds and illuminated the rippling water of the lake turning it to a golden syrup. The lake was huge and almost stretched beyond his eye could see. An hour ago, he was with the others escaping from the Chamber and now he was here - wherever that was.

He was in France. To be accurate, he was near the southern tip of La Lorraine in a town known as Gérardmer. Tom was not sure what time of day it was.

Tom walked forwards toward the lake. He was drawn by a faint ringing of bells.

Tramontane shouted, "Don't stray too far Tom." Tramontane had already swept the area in his mind and knew that the closest entity was a doe and her fawn about one kilometre north, so he allowed Tom to explore.

Mist rose from the lake's golden surface. Water dripped from the leaves of the trees around him and circulated around the rocks beneath his feet.

Aside from the greys and browns of the rocks, his surroundings were a complete spectrum of brilliant green. It was blinding. As if he were walking amongst emeralds.

He moved through the trees cautiously following what seemed like a well-trodden path. Tom was wearing his favourite high top all black converse. The soles were flat and not suited to the terrain.

Suddenly, his right foot slipped off a rock and into a gap, causing him to twist and fall frontwards into the edge of the lake. The water was shallow, and Tom's face collided with the lake bottom grazing his forehead. He rolled to one side lifting his head out of the water and sat up dazed. He composed himself and planted his hands on the lake bottom ready to stand.

As he did so, his right forefinger was pricked by a sharp pointed object. He looked down to see something glimmering below the surface of the water.

He reached down and lifted what appeared to be jewellery. At first, he thought it to be a broach but as he pulled it from the water, he realised it was a necklace as the chain unravelled from the pebbles.

Hanging from the necklace was a pendant - an opaque hexagonal crystal. Its clasp and the chain appeared to be made from gold.

No sooner had Tom drawn it from beneath the water but the chain wound its way around Tom's arm and snaked its way up under his sleeve fastening itself around his neck. Then, it pulled itself tight enough for the crystal to hang just above his chest bone and Tom felt the pendant lock itself to his skin.

The crystal began to shine green - first a light hue and gradually intensifying to a brilliant emerald.

Tom felt something stir inside him moving from the tips of his toes through his legs and torso up to his head. His eyes closed and he slumped backwards into the shallow water. He lay immersed at the bottom of the lake facing upwards and breathing quite normally.

Tramontane had sensed Tom's fall and was now standing above him. He grabbed Tom's arm to lift him from the water and immediately felt a surge of energy run through his body which forced him to let go as Tom lay back underwater.

He tried to lift him again but was once more repelled by a surge of energy which this time threw him backwards.

"Maestro!" yelled Tramontane.

Maestro appeared with Zoe at her side.

"What is this?" Maestro enquired. "Stay right back Zoe," she said as she lent forward to lift Tom from the water.

But another surge of energy burst from Tom's body and flung Maestro across the water beyond Tramontane.

Tramontane glanced back at Maestro who raised her hand to signal that she was OK and then he advanced towards Tom. He could see Tom breathing. As Tramontane peered closer, he realised Tom was growing at an extraordinary rate.

This cannot be? Tramontane thought. The transition between the Emissaries and the new generation had begun in the Chamber but the evolution to a fully grown Emissary took years and needed to be triggered by a charm. Then Tramontane saw the crystal pendant sparkling on Tom's chest.

Charms were hidden around the globe. Each charm was bespoke and destined for a specific Emissary. Eight at a time were made by the Master Jewellers at the Warden's request. The Warden imbued them with power, and they were then passed to the Custodians. Custodians mostly resided in recluse awaiting their calling to reveal the charm to its Emissary.

Zoe stood helplessly at the water's edge. If Tramontane and Maestro could do nothing, what could she do?

However, driven by impetuosity, Zoe dashed into the water before Tramontane or Maestro could prevent her.

"Stop Zoe!" Maestro screamed, lifting her hand and letting out a gentle blast of air to deter Zoe advancing further.
But it was too late.

Zoe had already reached Tom and was bending down into the water to grab him. She hesitated slightly when she realised that he had changed.

Suddenly, Tom extended his arm and clutched Zoe's hand. He drew his legs up to his body and with his other arm pushed himself from the water as his clothes fell away from his body. As Tom rose, Zoe looked upon him in silence. Tramontane and Maestro did likewise. He was almost unrecognisable. He had aged. His frame and height had more than doubled in size.

Tom staggered and was caught by Tramontane. Tramontane reached into his bag and took out a hooded cloak and sandals similar to the one he and Maestro wore.

"We had better cover you up Tom," he said. And Zoe blushed.

Tramontane recognised the pendant to be Tom's charm but it should have been stored away safely by the Custodians and wondered how it had come to be in the open and so close to them.

"It was Madame Vauqelin's doing," Tom spoke.

His voice had become much deeper.

"She left it there a few days ago. She had foreseen the attack on the Sanctuary but there was nothing she could have done to stop it. She knew we would find it. We must get to the château as soon as we can. The Wiccan is amassing her army."

Tramontane and Maestro understood. Tom had made his evolution to becoming an Emissary and was psychically linked to all things of the Sanctuary both past and present. The water in the lake had acted as a catalyst.

Tramontane was his mentor and Tom was his successor. Things were moving very quickly now. Tramontane pondered how he was going to be able to train Tom so quickly? At least the château would provide them with the shelter needed to do so.

CHAPTER 23

Bienvenus Mes Amis!

The trek through the woods lasted a full day but finally through a clearing the four saw the château in the distance.

It was the château de Bruyères.

The château was built by the Duke of Lorraine during the 10th century. The Duke had been one of the first Custodians in the Society.

Much of the château had been destroyed by fire in the 17th century and the ruins were a tourist spot. No one but the Duke's ancestors and the Sanctuary knew that the château extended far beyond the ruins of the outer walls into the hillside and were disguised by vegetation and trees.

The four climbed the hillside approaching the château to the side of the ruins so as to avoid the winding path used by tourists and locals alike.

They reached a small cemetery enclosed by a black twisted and rusted metal spoked fence. Within the cemetery lay twelve grave stones - one for each of Dukes of Lorraine and Custodians over the centuries.

The four moved through the cemetery and arrived at a chantry chapel beyond the graveyard. It was a simple square design with a large wooden door. Above the door the words *'Maison Lorraine'* were carved in stone, barely visible by erosion of time.

Tramontane turned the door's thick iron ring handle and it creaked on its hinges as he pushed it ajar.

The entrance to the chantry was so low that even Zoe had to duck as she entered to fit under the doorframe.

The space inside was bare and the air was moist. Water dripped down the stone walls and moss grew out of every aperture, but one thing was remarkable. On the ceiling was a large carving. One with which Tom and Zoe had become very familiar - the eight-pointed compass.

Tramontane hugged the wall as he moved to the back of the chantry and so the others followed.

It seemed as if Tramontane were sinking into the floor until the hood of his cloak passed under the back wall. In fact, he was simply descending steps. They were invisible to the eye because of their construction. Made of the same stone to the floor they sloped very gently to disguise them.

"Go on," Maestro said to Tom and Zoe.

And they followed Tramontane's footsteps until they had all disappeared under the chantry.

They found themselves in front of another door. This one was made of cast iron on which was welded a coat of arms. A crowned eagle with spread wings stood aloft another crown from which flowed leafs surrounding a striped shield inlaid with three more smaller eagles.

Tramontane knocked once. He waited ten seconds and then knocked twice. He waited ten seconds and then knocked three times.

"J'arrive!" a voice shouted.

There was shuffling behind the door and then the clink and clunk of metal as the door was unlocked from the inside.

It seemed endless, Tom thought. How many locks were on this door?

Finally, the door was pulled open and there stood a very short woman indeed with piercing black eyes, jet black hair which ran to her shoulders and a wispy black goatee beard. Several hooped piercings ran down the edge of both ears.

She looked up at Tramontane and Maestro and then Tom and Zoe behind them.

"Bienvenus mes amis!" they said. "Entrez donc."

The four stepped through the doorway into the most beautiful sitting room Tom and Zoe had ever seen.

The walls were dressed in silk and the floor was covered in the most intricately woven wool rugs. The lighting was sombre but highlighted the gold fittings and ornaments throughout.

"Faites comme chez-vous. How do you say it? Make yourselves at home. We have a lot to go through and very little time."

"Who are you?" demanded Zoe tired of the journey without any resolution.
"Your Custodian, I am Archduke Guillaume Lorraine. And you must be Zoe, no?" the woman replied. "

I do hope you're ready my dear, please come with me. Tom,

please join us.

She led both into an adjoining library.

It was oval shaped, and the walls were covered from floor to ceiling in books. Two wooden step ladders hung on a rail circling the room.

The Archduke manoeuvred the step ladder around the rail until they brought it to a stop.

"Le voilà!" she said.

They climbed to the top and fingered the spines of several books counting them as they went until they arrived at a brown thread hardback with gold trim. They pulled it from the shelf and descended. They then crossed the room to the other ladder and manoeuvred it to the exact opposite position to the first ladder. Once again, they climbed, and this time pulled a very large brown leather-bound book from the shelf.

They moved to the centre of the room and placed the books on a large mahogany table.

"Bon, alors. En premier, le bracelet."

They opened the brown thread book. It was, in fact, a box disguised as a book. They reached inside and drew out a bracelet. It appeared to be made of gold like the other charms. It was inlaid with a thorny twine which wrapped the entire bracelet and was topped with an unusual lily flower.

"Le Fleur-de-Lis, mademoiselle." said the Archduke. "A very powerful symbol my dear. Faith, wisdom, and chivalry. You see the thorns. The flower is the lily amongst the thorns. The lily is a sign of absolute purity in every sense. Pure of heart, pure of mind, pure of body. Your role has already been given to you ma chérie. You are his friend, his counsel and his protector."

"Who's?" asked Zoe, a bit bemused.

"Tom" said the Archduke.

Tom and Zoe looked at each other awkwardly.

"Bon. Let us move into the sitting room. This needs to be done properly and after all you have some friends to meet. I'm sure they are keeping good company with Tramontane and Maestro."

All three filed out of the library and into the sitting room. The open fireplace was crackling. Tramontane and Maestro stood either side of the fireplace and in front of them lay two very very big cats, rolling, purring, and preening themselves in the warmth of the fire.

"Meet Freya and Skadi. They are members of the Great Cats. They will follow you wherever you venture. Always by your side."

Freya was a Siberian Tiger and Skadi was a Brazilian Jaguar. Of course, they were not of the ordinary variety. They were blessed with extraordinary powers - like all the Great Cats.

Freya rose from her slumber and sloped across the room towards Tom. She was one of the largest of the pack. Her eyes were a sparkling blue almost human like. She looked up at Tom and purred.

Then she rubbed her jowls against his legs and feet and rolled onto her back inviting Tom to tickle her tummy. Tom bent down and obliged.

Freya purred more until Tom heard a voice. "Hello, thank you", it spoke with undulating tones. Then Freya looked into Tom's eyes. Tom heard the voice again. "Thank you, my Emissary. I am Freya, your protector."

"Thank you, Freya, I am pleased to meet you." Tom thought. Freya's eyes closed and her whiskers rose as if she were smiling. She growled gently and sloped back to the open fire before settling down next to Skadi.

Skadi had not moved. She knew that Zoe was to be her Emissary, but her evolution had not yet begun. Zoe had been stunned into silence by the cats' presence which was perfectly understandable. They were very menacing to look at but completely harmless to those around them.

"Take a seat, ma chérie", the Archduke said to Zoe. She pulled the bracelet from her pocket. Zoe instinctively raised her right arm and presented her wrist. The Archduke slid the bracelet carefully over her hand and onto her wrist. The bracelet drew itself tight against Zoe's skin. Zoe felt very nauseous at that moment. She could feel her blood pulsating through her veins and her temperature rising.

"I feel terribly sick", she said.

"That's quite normal. Some tea, perhaps?" the Archduke proffered.

"I think I need to rest. Perhaps lie down."

"Mais, bien sûr ma chérie. There are several guest bedrooms upstairs. Skadi will show you."

Skadi rose and sloped over to Zoe. Unlike Tom, Zoe had not grown and so Skadi's head reached Zoe's shoulders. "Lean against me, my Emissary", a voice said gently.

Zoe held Skadi's back as the two climbed the staircase. Skadi chose the nearest of the bedrooms. Zoe collapsed on the bed and Skadi jumped up and settled next to her purring. Zoe threw her arm over Skadi's torso and the two fell fast asleep. This was the beginning of a beautiful and legendary relationship. They would become inseparable. Formidable warriors to the very end.

Downstairs, the Archduke, Tom, Tramontane and Maestro sat at the dining table.

The Archduke had laid out some charcuterie, cheese, fresh bread, butter, and tomatoes. "I grow the tomatoes myself", he announced proudly. "I have 30 varieties. What would you like to drink?"

Tramontane and Maestro joined the Archduke in a glass of red wine and Tom opted for the homemade lemonade.

Freya lapped at a large bowl of water and crunched on one of two large marrow bones which the Archduke had saved especially for the cats' visit.

"Bon, allez, let's get started on this book. Zoe can catch up when she feels better."

It was the second of two original editions of the Compendium of Alchemists' Abstruse Contrivances. The first had been discovered by Alex in the library at Oxford.

The brown leather-bound book was in quite remarkable condition given its age.

The cover was embossed with a black lined Mandala. That is to say a geometric configuration of symbols and words. A large circle filled the cover. At its outer edge were all the signs of the zodiac and at each corner of the book were the words IGNIS (FIRE), AERIS (AIR), AQUAE (WATER) and TERRAE (EARTH).

Within the circle was a mountain upon which stood various regal and cavalier figures. The figures held an item in each hand.

The knights held a sword and shield. The kings and queens held sceptres and orbs. At either side of the foot of the mountain stood a male and female commoner. The male held a scythe and stem of wheat whilst the female cradled a baby.

On top of the mountain stood a much smaller figure - a boy perhaps. He held a star in one hand and a dagger in the other. Feathered wings protruded from his head and feet.

Within the mountain was a domed chamber. The sun was drawn on the left side of the dome and the moon was drawn on the right side. Both were depicted with faces which looked towards each other. Aloft the dome, stood a double headed eagle clutching a sword with its talons. Just above it was a bejewelled crown.

Within the chamber sat two figures holding plants and jars. They appeared to be in deep discussion.

Seven steps led up from the ground below to the foot of the mountain and entrance to the chamber. A word was carved in each step: caltination; sublimation; solution; putrefaction; distillation; coagulation and tinctur.

On the ground below stood a man with a cloth tied over his eyes. Around him was an abundance of flora and fauna.

"This is a wonderful book indeed. It was published in 1390 by Perenelle Flamel, wife of Nicolas Flamel. They were both alchemists and although Nicolas was arguably the most famous, in reality, it was Perenelle who was the most skilled and reputed. In fact, she was the Magister of the secret Alchemist's Circle during her later years. You see Alchemy is the study of the four elements - earth, air, fire, and water. Its focus has always been the transformation of matter. For centuries, alchemists were famed for pursuing the ultimate quest to transform lead into gold, but this had already been achieved by the great alchemists of Greco-Roman Egypt. However, it was a closely guarded secret known only to the Circle. The Circle held the knowledge to do so much more. Before her death, Perenelle Flamel documented formulae for various transformations in this compendium. They are all very impressive but quite ordinary. Party pieces for mere entertainment. However, the secret is in the title itself - "The Compendium of Alchemists' Abstruse Contrivances". The book is a collection of artificial creations which obscure its true contents. The secret of life and death and all that lies between. The divine and the mortal. The spiritual and the material. The infinite and the infinitesimal. The beginning and the end. La jouissance et la douleur. I mean great happiness and great sadness. This book contains immense power which must be used wisely and protected above all else. It has not been possible until now to unlock its contents but now we have la clé."

"La clé?" asked Tom.

"Désolé mon ami, the key," the Archduke answered.

"What is the key?" Tom enquired.

The Archduke chuckled to themselves and Tramontane and Maestro both drew wry smiles.

"WHO is the key would be more precise, Tom," Why, YOU are the key Tom. It is YOU, my boy."

CHAPTER 24

Our Prattling Father

Alexander and Stephen emerged from the tunnel through a tiny hatch with Emissaries Grecale and Ostro by their side.

"This is nuts!" Stephen declared.

"I totally agree!" Alexander replied. "Where on earth are we?" he enquired.

Their surroundings were very different to those of Tom and Zoe. They were standing under a very large gateway clouded by fog. It was nighttime.

Stephen recognised the architecture almost immediately. He wasn't far from his office. "We're in London. The City of London. Isn't this St. John's Gate?" he said.

"Yes, it is indeed." said Grecale. "The church is nearby. Move quickly and stay close."

Grecale peered out from under the gateway. He sensed danger lurking in the shadows. He moved swiftly across the cobbled yard. Stephen and Alexander followed. Ostro came last.

Both Ostro and Grecale sensed that an attack was imminent, but they needed to keep moving and get Stephen and Alexander to the church and safety.

They headed up St. John's Lane. The sound of horse hoofs striking the pavement and neighing followed behind them.

"That sounds like horses?" Alexander enquired.

"That's trouble." Grecale said bluntly. "Step up your pace. The church isn't far."

They turned into St. John Street as the noise of horse hoofs and neighing grew in intensity. It was joined by a screeching whistling.

"Cover your ears and don't look back! Keep moving forward!"

They had arrived at Charterhouse Street next to Smithfield Market.

"The church is just on the other side of the marketplace." said Grecale.

But he knew they would need to make a stand now. There was no way Stephen and Alexander would make it to the church without confronting the riders.

All at once, Grecale and Ostro came together shrouding Stephen and Alexander under their capes which seemed to triple in size as they covered them.

The marketplace was normally full of traders and stalls but now it was empty. Grecale and Ostro lifted their staffs and struck the ground which shuddered under the force of their impact.

The shock waves revealed the horses and their riders. They were the same as encountered by Tramontane at the museum.

The horses were twenty hands high and black. Their eye sockets were empty. Their riders seemed to twist and flicker changing form constantly.

Grecale and Ostro struck the ground with their staffs once more and raised their hands in unison towards the sky. The roofs of the marketplace rattled as a small, concentrated cyclone appeared above them.

The horses reared and tried desperately to keep their footing. Their riders reached forwards with their hands trying to grab at the Emissaries. They shrieked and screamed as they were lifted towards the sky and pulled into the vacuum of the cyclone.

Grecale and Ostro lowered their hands and the vacuum closed. They lifted their cloaks. The two boys looked up at the Emissaries.

"What the bloody hell was that!" Alexander said.

"The Infernal", Ostro said. "The spirits of excommunicated knights with an insatiable lust for death."

"Let's get the Stephen and Alexander to the church Ostro." Grecale said.

They passed through the marketplace onto Rising Sun Court and up to the gated cloisters of the church of Saint Bartholomew the Great.

Grecale waved his hand over the padlocked chain on the gate, and it fell open. He pushed through into the courtyard and up to the main doors of the church.

Grecale knocked once. He waited ten seconds then knocked twice. He waited ten seconds and then knocked three times.

"What time do you call this?!" a very abrupt voice declared from inside the church.

The doors opened to reveal a very tall and spindly priest with a slight hunch and long white beard.

"Come in, come in. Welcome children. There's much to do. Come on now. Lots to do. No time. Are you hungry, thirsty? You must be famished, parched! Let's get you into the warm. Settle you down. Yes, there's a lot to do. No time. So sorry to hear about Madame Vauqelin. How sad. How terribly sad. How terribly, terribly sad. Follow me now, lots to do. No time. Poor Madame Vauqelin. Poor poor Madame Vauqelin."

"I'm Alexander…" Alexander began to say.

"And he is Stephen", the priest said. "Yes, yes. I know who you are and why you're here. I mean, you must be here. You must be here. It's where you must be, now. Right now. Here. Right here. I'm Father Raherius. Not the Father Raherius of course. He died almost 900 years ago. Funny man he was. I'm told. I didn't know him of course. I mean how could I? He's long since dead and buried. Apparently, he never stopped talking. Never stopped. I mean, how irritating. Can you imagine? Never stopped. You could not get a word in edgeways. I mean, so I'm told. A very funny man. A favourite of King Henry I you know. A jester and a minstrel, I'm told, as well as being a monk. I mean, can you imagine that?! A man of God telling jokes and singing songs. I never. Anyway, I did hear a good joke the other day. What was it now? Oh, I can't remember. Oh, hee hee. I just thought. How funny. I play the organ and I sing in our choir! How funny. How funny. Hee hee. I guess I'm no different to old Father Raherius. Founded the **Priory of the Hospital of St Bartholomew** back in 1123. Built this church you know. Not literally, I mean. Builders did that. Designed it. Yes, designed it. What a clever fellow. Yes, very clever fellow. How clever. Anyway, what was I saying? Oh, yes. Lots to do. No time. Enough of this prattling you two. No time for prattling. No time for prattling. Lots to do, you know. Lots to do. Follow me. Follow me. No dawdling!"

And with that Father Raherius scuttled off down the aisle.

Stephen and Alexander looked at each other with a wry smile on their faces. Grecale and Ostro looked at them.

"Yes, yes. He's quite the character" said Grecale. "But please do exactly as he says. He's your Custodian."

"What are you doing, children! Prattling. That's what!" Father Raherius shouted from the altar. "Were you not listening to me? No time. No time. Stop your prattling. No prattling. Hop to it!"

With that, all four followed Father Raherius to the back of the church and into the Vestry.

Once inside, Father Raherius closed and locked the door to the Vestry.

The Vestry was rather modest in size (compared to the rest of the church) but very neatly designed.

A bench ran the length of all four wood-panelled walls. It was partitioned into individual seats and above each seat was a cubby hole and below a name plate and hook upon which each church chorister hung their cassock.

Father Raherius said, "Make way, coming through!" to the four who stood in the middle of the room wondering where they were going next.

Father Raherius headed to his seat and pulled the hook down. It locked into position. He proceeded to push the left partition across the bench and the wood panel behind the bench moved with it. He did the same on the right to expose an opening behind the Vestry. He reached inside and flicked a switch.

"I imagine that you're becoming used to tunnels now children. Hee hee! London's riddled with them you know. Not just the Tube, my dears. Hundreds of them you know. I'm surprised the city doesn't just sink into them. Poof! Like that." he made a gesture with his hands imitating a magician performing a trick. "Do you want to know where this one leads? Should I tell you or shall we wait to find out. A surprise. Yes, a surprise. I do love surprises. Follow me. Not time to waste. No time for prattling you know. How you children do prattle. Non-stop isn't it! Prattle, prattle, prattle. Oh, my dear me. You must stop it." And with that, Father Raherius scuttled through the opening and into the tunnel.

"I suppose we should follow him", Tom said.

"Absolutely," Grecale replied.

They all stepped into the tunnel.

"Draw those panels to please!" Father Raherius shouted from a distance. And Ostro duly obliged.

They walked about five hundred metres and emerged into a very large crypt. Father Raherius moved slowly through the crypt passing from one Chamber to another.

"I never remember which Chamber it's in. Never could you know. It's in the big Chamber, I think. Where is it? Not this Chamber."

There were several Chambers housing ornate tombs. Eventually, they arrived at the largest of all the Chambers so far - Nelson's Chamber.

"Are we under St. Paul's Cathedral?" Stephen enquired.

"Yes, yes my dear boy." Father Raherius replied. "Well spotted. Vice-Admiral Horatio Nelson's Chamber. Ah, yes of course. Now I remember. That's his sarcophagus. 1st Viscount. 1st Duke of Bronte. Knight Companion of the Most Honourable Order of the Bath. *TRIA JUNCTA IN UNO*."

"Three joined in one," Alexander interjected.

"Indeed, indeed," said Father Raherius. You know your Latin. Well done. Well done. Horatio was a friend of the Society you see. A Great Mariner. A friend. Did you know he suffered from seasickness? It dogged him all his life. Imagine that - the greatest naval officer suffered from seasickness! Hee hee."

Grecale and Ostro looked at each other. They sensed a subtle change in the atmosphere of the Crypt. A shifting of time. Very slight.

"Father Raherius, we need to hurry," Grecale emphasised.

"Ah, yes, you're absolutely right. No time for prattle young Alexander. Let's get on with it. Boys, I need your assistance. Please take these."

He reached into a small pouch hanging from a string around his neck and pulled out three large coins. Each coin was pressed with the same image of three imperial crowns within a circle in which the motto *TRIA JUNCTA IN UNO* was inscribed. Father Raherius handed one to Stephen and one to Alexander.

"Alexander, you stand at the head of the sarcophagus and Stephen you stand at the foot."

The boys did as they were instructed.

"Now you will see a similar design to that on your coin on the sarcophagus. It's the Civil Knight Grand Cross Star of the the Most Honourable Order of the Bath

The boys both saw the design. This time in red and gold with rays of silver issuing from the centre.

Father Raherius was standing to one side of the sarcophagus looking at the third star on the side.

"Three joined in one," he said and chuckled. "Place the coins on the stars."

The boys did as they were told.

"Now, on the count of three, push the coins. England expects every man to do his duty! Hee hee. One, two, three.

All three pushed the coins.

There was a clunk and a small compartment slid open at the base of the sarcophagus where Father Raherius stood. He reached inside and took out a red velvet parcel tied with a thick red ribbon. The materials were slightly faded.

Father Raherius untied the parcel to reveal a ring. It was gold and on its top in a clasp a roughly cut opaque crystal.

Grecale and Ostro moved closer to Father Raherius and the boys as the temperature in the Crypt fell and the echoes of furious whispering ran through the Chambers around them.

"Father, we need to move this along please," said Grecale.

With that Father Raherius advanced towards Alexander. "Are you right or left-handed?" he shouted.

"Right-handed."

He grabbed Alexander's right hand and thrust the ring onto his middle finger. He waited an instant then removed the ring. "Not you then."

He moved swiftly to Stephen and shouted, "Right or Left?"

"Left," Stephen replied anxiously.

Father Raherius grabbed his right hand. As he started to position the ring next to his middle finger it flew forward and slid itself to the bottom of Stephen's finger. Stephen felt the ring tighten slightly clasping itself to his skin. Then the crystal began to glow.

"To thine own self be true", Father Raherius said. "Tom has evolved and so will you, Stephen". Father Raherius gave Stephen a soothing smile.

Stephen started to shake violently as the whispering rose to an unbearable level.

Grecale and Ostro knew there was no way they would all escape now.

Then, Stephen's body began to flicker - disappearing and re-appearing. He was shifting in time. "What is happen... happen... happening to m...m... me?!" he stuttered between flickers.

Alexander stood aghast, not knowing what to do or say. It was an extraordinary sight and the whispering had turned to shrieking.

He covered his ears to protect them as much as he could from the cacophony.

"Try to stay calm Stephen," Grecale said in a reassuring voice. But Grecale understood the predicament. They couldn't leave until Stephen had adjusted to his new existence but if they stayed, they would surely be overwhelmed by what was about to enter the crypt.

Then, Stephen saw the small man dressed in a threadbare black suit with bloodshot eyes who had appeared before him at the railway station.

He had emerged through a wall to the side of the Chamber and was staring directly at Stephen with a chilling regard. One by one, he pointed his long sinewy index finger at everyone in the Chamber and then drew his finger across his eyes.

"The... They... They're here!" Stephen stuttered. "The Unremembered!"

Father Raherius knew there was nothing he could do but shelter Alexander.

"Oh dear, oh dear, the Unremembered. Very nasty bunch. Sneaking through the cracks. No time. Alexander, come here quickly!" he shouted.

Grecale and Ostro confirmed, "Go Alexander!"

Father Raherius started to push the sarcophagus.

"I need your help!" he said.

Alexander arrived by his side and pushed but the weight was too heavy.

With one gesture, Grecale lifted his hand and instantly the sarcophagus was sent smashing across the Chamber.

"Leave now!" Grecale cried. Father Raherius and Alexander descended into the vault below. "Poor Nelson," Father Raherius muttered.

Then Grecale and Ostro joined hands to create an immense gale directed exactly where the small man stood but he didn't move, let alone flinch.

The walls around them began to shudder.

And then they emerged - sickly, gaunt figures of all ages (children and adults alike) dressed in Victorian clothing and chanting, "You don't belong here, get out, get away, be gone with you!".

The Unremembered had crossed not just time but dimension. In our time, in our dimension they were extremely dangerous and Grecale and Ostro were just not strong enough to deter them.

Stephen stopped flickering and shifting in time. He realised that he had adapted to and gained control of his newfound form. He had been drawn to the Unremembered before or rather they had been drawn to him.

There was a connection between him and these visitors. If they crossed over permanently, it would bring a curse on the world from which there would be no return. Slowly but surely they would move from home to home turning everyone and everything into a forgotten relic. Forever lost as if no one or thing had ever existed.

Stephen began edging forwards towards the small man who began furiously hissing and spitting at Stephen.

Grecale shouted, "Stephen, stop, it's too soon. You'll be lost. We won't be able to find you."

Stephen could hear Grecale's muffled exclamation, but his mind was focussed on the Unremembered.

"You don't belong here, you get out, you get away, be gone with you!" Stephen chanted. "You don't belong here, you get out, you get away, be gone with you! You don't belong here, you get out, you get away, be gone with you!" he repeated over and over as his voice rose to an extraordinary volume.

Now every man and child were hissing and spitting at Stephen as he edged ever closer.

The small man recoiled as Stephen pressed the Unremembered back. They sensed his connection and feared his presence. But they would not leave. Stephen knew what he had to do. The only way to send them back from whence they came was to return with them. He launched himself into their horde.

They were without substance. Reflections and shadows of people long since passed. They swirled around Stephen as he heard the echoes of their voices. "He's one of us now," they said.

But they hadn't realised what Stephen had done in that moment. He had drawn them back away from the Crypt, away from St. Paul's, away from London, away from everything in our time and space back to the railway station and that dark dusty waiting room where he had first encountered them.

By the time they noticed, it was too late. They clawed and kicked, throwing their arms forward in desperation to cling onto time and pull themselves back into the Crypt but it was to no avail. They all returned to the waiting room with Stephen. Once inside, the door slammed shut and the screams became whimpering. "What has he done, what has he done?" the voices moaned in the darkness.

Then, a new voice, one Stephen had never heard before, announced itself. "Quiet, you pathetic creatures!" it demanded. "Clever boy," it said with a somewhat prurient tone. "You must show me how you did that."

Stephen peered into the darkness towards the voice. Try as he might the room was in permanent blackness.

Then she stepped forward and stroked the back of his hand with her nail moving slowly down towards the ring. "Ah, now I see," she said. She moved close to Stephen's side and whispered in his ear. "I am the Wiccan and you, well you... you are my first."

CHAPTER 25

Goodbye Mum and Dad

Mr. Waldly walked briskly down the street. The metal taps on his handmade Church's oxford shoes made a sharp clicking sound against the pavement.

Charlie followed close behind distracted by that sound. After a few moments, they turned off Floral Street and emerged onto James Street heading towards the market at Covent Garden.

"Please Mr. Waldly, what is going on? I need to get back home and let my parents know that I'm safe," Charlie said.

"Absolutely, my dear. But first we must find somewhere safe for you."

As they crossed the cobble stones, the sound made by Mr. Waldly's metal taps grew louder and echoed across the square until Charlie realised that the echoes were not echoes at all but a second and third set of footsteps.

"Mr. Waldly, I think we're being followed." Charlie said tentatively.

"We are definitely being followed. They've been on us since we left the newsagent." Mr. Waldly replied. "We'll be safe once we get to the hotel. It's on the far side of the market. We need to get off this court. We're too exposed. Into the crowds. This way!"

It was a late Saturday evening. Many of the shops were still open and the bars were full of revellers.

Mr. Waldly and Charlie made their way into the market buildings. As they did so, Charlie caught sight of their pursuers.

Two men dressed in dark suits with turtleneck jumpers. They were as wide as they were tall. They had quickened their pace and gained ground moving closer and closer.

"We're not going to reach the hotel unless we lose them," Mr. Waldly said. "Down here!"

They descended some steps into the yard below. A trio of buskers were playing Bach to a small crowd of onlookers. Behind the crowd was a small museum of automata.

"In here, I know the owner."

"Mr. Waldly! Well, I never!" said a jovial voice. "What are you doing here my old friend?"

"Mr. Charles, we need some help. Somewhere to hide a moment if you would."

Mr. Charles ushered them to the back of the museum into his office.

"There is a door on the other side," he said. Rest here a while. "If anyone comes looking for you. I'll make a signal. I'll turn on all the automata. They make quite the racket you know!"

A few minutes later, Mr. Charles heard a commotion outside. One of the pursuers had tripped over the buskers' case and knocked the crowd's donations across the cobbled stones.

They pushed through the crowds and into the pub opposite

the museum looking left and right as they moved. Then they emerged from the pub and pushed through the crowds again making their way towards the museum.

Mr. Charles was sitting on a stall just outside his office. He reached down and pulled at a red metal lever on the wall.

All at once, every automaton came to life. Small and large. Each giving its own performance. The noise was so loud it drowned out the trio outside who stopped playing. A little boy and his mother ran out of the museum with their hands over their ears.

The two men stopped in their tracks and hesitated to come further into the museum.

Mr. Waldly and Charlie opened the second door and exited the office into the adjoining courtyard. They ran up the steps onto the ground level and hurried forward through the antiques and crafts of Jubilee Market onto Tavistock Street.

"We're almost there!" Mr. Waldly declared.

By now, the two men had left the museum and were still scouting Covent Garden Market. But the trail had gone cold.

Mr. Waldly and Charlie proceeded onto Exeter Street and then emerged onto the Strand.

"Ah, there she is. The beauty!" exclaimed Mr. Waldly pointing to the Savoy across the road. We'll be safe there.

The two crossed the Strand and walked down Savoy Court. As they approached the door, the porter recognised Mr. Waldly.

"Hello, sir. Lovely to see you again." He spoke into his lapel. "Mr. Waldly is here."

The hotel manager greeted Mr. Waldly and Charlie by the desk.

"Your usual room Mr. Waldly and one for your guest?"

"Yes, please." Mr. Waldly replied.

The manager led them into the lift. He inserted a key and pressed the 'basement level' button. The lift shuddered and then started moving. It didn't seem to Charlie that it was going down or indeed up but sideways.

It was a short journey and when the lift doors opened, they found themselves standing in the most charming hexagonal glass conservatory filled with exotic plants. At each edge was a door.

"You're not allergic, are you, young lady? We can have them removed if you wish. They were an old favourite of King Edward VII. He used to insist on them every time he stayed with us. Churchill loved them too. It became a tradition like most of these things. Anyhow, you'll be quite safe here. There's only one way in and out. The glass is mirrored so no one can see you from above but you can enjoy the sky view. Through that door is the balcony to our theatre. We have four bedrooms. I believe Mr. Waldly will be choosing that one. He pointed across the conservatory but you are free to choose any of the other three."

"Thank you, very much," Charlie said. "What is behind that door?"

"Ah, the sixth door. Well, I am not allowed in there but I am sure Mr. Waldly will explain it to you.

"But you're the hotel manager?" Charlie pointed out.

"Yes, indeed. But whatever is behind that door is not my concern young lady. Some things must remain a secret. I wasn't sure how long you were staying so I thought a buffet with cold beverages might be in order. I will have them delivered via the dumb waiter. If there's anything you need, just phone me. Oh, you will also find an assortment of clothes in each wardrobe. I do hope you will find something to your size and taste. You can imagine that the style here is somewhat traditional."

With that, the hotel manager went back into the lift.

"Right, first things first. Let's call your parents." Mr. Waldly stated.

Charlie reached for the handset to the black Bakelite rotary dial phone which sat on a trestle-based teak coffee table in the centre of the conservatory and dialled home.

"Mum, it's me. I'm OK."

"Oh darling, we were so worried. You disappeared by the old arcade. Everyone's been out looking for you. What happened? Where are you sweetheart?"

"Is that Charlie? Oh, thank God!" Charlie heard her father say in the background.

"Well, it's a little difficult to explain but I'm with a very nice man Mr. Waldly and we're trying to find somebody called a Emissary."

"Oh, oh… It's begun already." Charlie's mother said. "We knew you weren't far off but… Oh, my darling Charlie. I wanted to see you, sweetheart before…"

"Before what mum?"

"Well, before you change sweetie." Charlie's mother choked on her words, struggling to speak. Tears fell from her eyes. She drew a deep breath and continued. Charlie just listened in silence wondering what her mother was talking about.

"Mum, are you crying?"

"A little, my angel. But don't worry. We knew this time would come."

"What do you mean? What time? Why will I change?"

"We've known since you were a tiny baby. We were told. Now, listen to me very carefully. Mr. Waldly will take good care of you but you must find your Emissary and the Custodian.

"Custodian? What do you mean? How do you know so much?"

Charlie's father drew close to his wife and the earpiece not wanting to disrupt the precious time Charlie had with her mother.

"Sweetheart, daddy loves you so much. I love you. Now, you must go. We will see each other again soon…"

"I love you mum. I love you dad." And with that Charlie's mother hung up the telephone.

Charlie did the same. She was close to tears herself. Her parents knew. Probably, more than she did. She turned to Mr. Waldly who was now standing discreetly in the corner.

"Try to rest, my dear. The next twenty-four hours are going to feel like a whirlwind. I must try to reach Madame again. We need to get you to your Emissary and Custodian as soon as possible."

Mr. Waldly lifted the handset to the black Bakelite rotary dial phone. He dialled the Society's number 4321 123 4321 several times but the call would not connect.

"Something is very wrong," he said. We won't be able to linger too long. Just then a small bell rang above the dumb waiter. Mr. Waldly opened its door and removed the trays of food and drink placing them on a matching dining table.

"Alas, a light supper and refresh and then we must move on. Such a shame. I would have loved to watch the show. It's one of my favourites - Gilbert and Sullivan's H.M.S Pinafore. It's such a hoot!"

Mr. Waldly and Charlie picked at the buffet. Neither were particularly hungry. Then both retired to their rooms to freshen up.

Charlie pondered the very strange day she was having. This morning she had been competing on the South Coast, then found herself in that ghostly arcade, then was chased through Covent Garden and now was in the Savoy hotel! And her parents knew something.

She looked through the wardrobe. The manager was right. It was all very traditional - more Mr. Waldly's style than her own. She decided her running clothes and trainers were much more practical. Especially if they were going to be pursued again! They were.

She emerged from her room a few hours later. Mr. Waldly was sitting in one of the velour wingback chairs sipping on a cup of darjeeling tea.

"Who were those men Mr. Waldly? What did they want? What is going on?" Charlie enquired.

"They're henchmen. I don't mean to unnerve you but you don't seem the type anyway. They were after you," Mr. Waldly replied.

"Me? Why me?"

"Well, you're special my dear. Madame was meant to explain all of this to you but she's not around. Oh dear, I need to get you to your Emissary and Custodian. They will do a far better job at explaining all of this than me! This is not how it was meant to be at all! Most unsatisfactory! Now, we're going to step through that sixth door shortly. Do you remember how we left the shop and appeared in Mr. Singh's newsagent? Well, it's going to be a similar experience. I'm not entirely sure where we're going. This wasn't meant to be my role you see. You need to be with your Emissary and I don't know where they are. Hopefully, they'll find you soon. Right then, nothing left but to open that door."

Mr. Waldly picked up a brown leather carry bag which he had prepared for the next part of their journey. Charlie stood to his side.

Mr. Waldly checked the time on his watch. "Would you like to do the honours?" he invited.

Charlie clasped the brass doorknob and turned it until the door became loose in its frame. Mr. Waldly gave her a reassuring smile.

Charlie opened the door to reveal a blindingly white void in front of them. They both stepped back so Charlie could open the door wide and then stepped forward through the door into the void. The door shut behind them.

CHAPTER 26

Azarflame

They reappeared among what seemed to be rugs hanging all around.

They could hear the sound of bells, the chatter of voices and the humming of small engines. They could smell spices wafting through the air.

Mr. Waldly pushed through the rugs and Charlie followed.

They emerged into a small cabin shaded from the bright sunshine outside. Rugs hung from the walls and lay across the floor piled high.

At the entrance of the cabin sat an old man dressed in a white gown wearing sandals. As they approached, he turned to look at them. Mr. Waldly had expected him to be surprised but far from it the old man was delighted to see them.

He had a dark complexion with wrinkled sun-aged skin. As he smiled his wrinkles became more pronounced which in turn made his smile more pronounced. His eyes were a deep blue and exuded joy and kindness. He rose from his wooden stool slowly with the aid of a long stick.

He continued to look and smile at Mr. Waldly and Charlie.

He shut the shop front by closing the two doors and bolting them. Then, he folded a large hasp over its staple. Finally, he took a large padlock from a shelf and fed its shackle through the staple and fastened it tightly into its body. He pulled and shook the padlock a few times to make sure it was locked.

Mr. Waldly and Charlie looked on, saying nothing.

Then, he turned and walked between them through the rugs to the back of the shop, beckoning them as he moved slowly ahead, pushing his stick into the ground at every step. He opened a door which gave onto a very narrow alley running between the shop and the neighbouring building.

He waited for Mr. Waldly and Charlie to exit and then locked the door behind them. Then, he squeezed between them and made his way up the alley.

A slight breeze whipped up a cloud of sand from the ground.

The air was hot and Mr. Waldly quickly removed his jacket, placing it in his hold-all, and rolled up his sleeves. Charlie was wearing a short sleeve T-shirt and three-quarter length running tights and felt vindicated that she had chosen not to change her attire at the Savoy.

After they had passed several doors, the man stopped and knocked at a black metal door. It was old and rusted.

Immediately, a small shutter opened to reveal a spy hole through which a single eye peered and twitched, moving left to right and up and down. No sooner had it opened. it snapped shut.

Then, came a rattling of keys and clanging of metal as several keys were turned in locks and bolts were drawn open. It seemed like an age until finally the door was pulled open and a giant of a man grinned with crooked stained teeth and said, "As-salam-alaykom." to which the old man replied in kind.

Then, the giant spoke English. "Come in, quickly." All three obliged and the giant shut and locked the door behind them.

They stood in the atrium of the most beautiful oasis far removed from the outside. A fountain was running in its middle and the high ceiling and walls were tiled in shimmering aquamarine coloured mosaic on which the undulating water of the fountain reflected - making it seem as if the walls themselves were made of water. Tall palm trees sprouted from the ground and small multi-coloured birds sang jubilantly from their perches.

They crossed the atrium to an adjoining room.

It was equally decadent - an array of bright technicolour. Silk sheets adorned the walls and huge pillows adorned the floors.

The giant asked both Mr. Waldly and Charlie to remove their shoes.

Then, he reached into a cupboard and pulled out fresh pairs of silk slippers. Mr. Waldly and Charlie put on the slippers and were then beckoned into the room to sit wherever they were most comfortable as the giant moved back into the atrium to rejoin the old man closing the double doors behind him.

Mr. Waldly sat rather awkwardly on the large cushions and placed his hold-all by his side. Charlie remained standing.

A few minutes passed before the double doors on the other side of the room opened and in came a lady in a beautiful green linen gown carrying a silver tray with a porcelain teapot, four cups and saucers and a jar. She placed it on top of a wooden cabinet to the side. She poured the contents of the pot into each of the cups and discreetly left the room. Leaving the doors ajar. An odour of roses wafted across the room.

A very majestic lady entered the room. She was tall and wore a white silk dress tied at the waste by a purple cord. On her head, she wore a crystal tiara. Her eyes were chestnut brown and her auburn hair flowed behind her to the bottom of her back. Her lips were full, and her smile was utterly intoxicating.

"How do you do?" she said. "I am the Shahzadeh Mandana. Please, would you like some rose water. We have some Masghati if you would like it. It's a speciality of my hometown."

"Would you like some refreshment Charlotte… Mr. Waldly?"

"I would very much, thank you. How do you know my name?" Charlie enquired.

"Yes, please Shahzadeh Mandana," Mr Waldly said.

"I've been expecting you Charlotte," the Shahzadeh replied. I am a friend of the Society. Here to do all I can to help you.

"The preparations have been made Mr. Waldly. We leave tonight. But there has been no sign of the Emissary. Is that not strange?"

"Yes, it is odd. They should have found Charlie by now but she has shifted across dimensions, escaped the Unremembered and crossed two portals all in a day! Quite remarkable!" Mr. Waldly said.

"And don't forget those henchmen, Mr. Waldly!" Charlie reminded him.

"Yes, yes my dear. You're absolutely right."

"Well, I do apologise but we must deliver you to your Custodian. The sooner the better. They live on the other side of the valley beyond the mountains. The mountains are a dangerous place for anyone, but my escort should deliver you safely. And I will come with you, of course. It is the least I can do for the Society. It is best we travel at night under the cover of darkness. And it will be cooler."

As night time fell, the horses were led into the courtyard.

The Shahzadeh walked out dressed in brown leather trousers, boots and cropped top with a cape draped around her shoulders. On one arm was perched a bird of prey.

She was followed by four male escorts. They were also dressed from head to toe in leather. This time black. Each wore headscarves which only revealed their eyes. Each carried a variety of swords and blades of different shapes and sizes. The Persians were renowned for their weapons.

Mr. Waldly stood next to Charlie.

"I am a keen collector of ancient weapons," he said, "but never have I seen a collection like that. The Shamshir is reputed to be the finest of all swords in history. They are carrying every sort. Each has its own purpose: the Talwar; the Kilij; the Scimitar; the Sabre; the Khopesh; the Kukri, the Falchion... my god where are we going!"

"Have no fear," the Shahzadeh said reassuringly. You will be very safe with my royal guard and my favourite Shahbaz will be watching over us from the sky. She will let us know if there is anything dangerous lying in wait.

"But the Shahbaz are birds of fable," Mr. Waldly replied.

"And fables are stories - some true, some false. In this instance, the fable is true. The Shahbaz are very real, but their existence is kept secret. They are a small family. There are only twelve. This is Azarflame. She will guide us through Ghafghaz mountains. It is where she grew up. There is no better guide."

"Yalla!" she cried.

The bird opened its wings which spanned at least one and a half metres either side of its fleecy body. Its eyes were a vivid yellow with dilated black pupils. The bird turned to look at the Shahzadeh and then squawked loudly as it launched upwards. It climbed and climbed. Its body glistened in the moonlight. When it had reached about 3,000 feet it stopped and circled the group on the ground below.

"Do you ride?" the Shahzadeh enquired belatedly.

"I do!" Charlie replied enthusiastically.

"I don't," Mr. Waldly said rather sheepishly.

"Don't worry, these horses are very easy going. Mr. Waldly you can ride with me. Just hang onto my waist tightly."

Charlie gave Mr. Waldly a mischievous wink and he blushed as she mounted her horse.

The guards followed suit synchronously. Two took the lead and two moved to the rear.

Lastly, the Shahzadeh mounted, swivelled round and extended her arm to Mr. Waldly hoisting him up onto the horse. "Now remember, Mr. Waldly, hang onto tightly."

"Yes, madame." Mr. Waldly said as he held her waist.

"Tightly Mr. Waldly!" exclaimed the Shahzadeh. "I'm not having you fall off."

Mr. Waldly pulled closer to the Shahzadeh, acutely embarrassed.

"Very good. Now let's ride. We must make it before sunrise. Yalla!"

The Shahzadeh signalled to her guard and looked up to Azarflame who stopped circling, squawked, and headed north.

The group followed unaware of what was lying in wait or rather who.

They climbed through the rock-strewn mountains slowly and steadily. It was a gradual ascent at first but as they climbed higher the path became steeper. The horses wove between the boulders which littered the mountainsides. They were very sure footed and familiar with the terrain. The escort was on constant alert surveilling the land ahead.

"We will rest here," said the Shahzadeh. "It is unusually quiet."

"How so?" enquired Mr. Waldly.

"These mountains are full of criminals - thieves, assassins, traffickers… You name it, they're here. We should have come across some scoundrels by now. It's very odd. Something's not right. Everyone be on your guard. We won't stop for long."

The guards passed around flasks of water and passion fruit, and everyone drank and ate tentatively.

Azarflame hovered overhead gliding on the gentle night breeze. The moon shone brightly and reflected through the clouds onto the ground below.

Suddenly, Azarflame changed her flight. She drew her immense wings tightly to her body and began to dive. The pupils of her eyes shrunk to the size of tiny pinholes as she descended rapidly.

She had seen movement near the group. A strange apparition of a small cloud hidden behind the boulders. It gradually grew in size becoming larger and denser until it began to take shape and rose from the ground.

Azarflame let out a screeching cry to capture the attention of the group.

The guards immediately drew their weapons and the Shahzadeh lifted the longbow over her head and drew an arrow from its quiver onto the bow string pulling it taught in one fluid motion.

They formed a protective circle around Charlie and Mr. Waldly.

Mr Waldly furrowed his bag desperately trying to find something.

Charlie instinctively fell to one knee and pulled Mr. Waldly down with her.

The apparition rose higher until it revealed itself to the group. The cloud had turned a vivid black and dispersed outwards from the form inside.

Then, snake-like and sinewed fingers emerged from the cloud. Then, boney and scabbed hands. Then, long and thin arms. Then, a mouth which smiled in a sinister fashion revealing long stained sharp teeth. It clicked its middle fingers and thumbs and the cloud instantly fell away to reveal the Wiccan. She stopped smiling and fixed her eyes on the group below with a regard devoid of any emotion.

"Give her to me," she said. "And I might consider allowing you to die painlessly. Resist and not only will you die in excruciating pain the likes of which you could never imagine but in death you will suffer an eternity of torturous hell."

Azarflame had almost reached the Wiccan and had opened her wings to break her descent, as well as extending her feet and long sharp talons.

The Wiccan lifted her hand and caught Azarflame squarely around her throat. Azarflame squealed but lashed out with her talons cutting the Wiccan several times across the arm.

The Shahbaz's talons were reputed to be sharp enough to cut through anything. It was one of the reasons why they had been hunted almost to extinction.

The Wiccan winced in pain and released Azarflame who fell to the ground.

The guards threw a succession of blades and the Shahzadeh unleashed a flurry of arrows at the Wiccan. The Wiccan raised her hands toward the blades and arrows and moved them either side of her in a sweeping motion of her arms as they clattered against the rocks behind her.

Two of the guards advanced swiftly towards the Wiccan but could do nothing to her from the ground as she floated above their heads.

The Wiccan laughed as she lifted them from the ground with a further motion of her arms. They hung midair, flaying their arms and legs desperately trying to break free from the Wiccan's supernatural grip. In one effortless twist of her wrist, their thick necks were snapped like twigs and the Wiccan propelled their lifeless corpses back at the group who looked on in horror.

Mr. Waldly dug through his bag frantically. He had prepared for this moment but had not expected it to come so soon.

The guards and the Shahzadeh had tightened the circle around Charlie and Mr. Waldly. Both were on the ground. They heard the shrill cackling of the Wiccan and the heavy thud of the bodies landing in front of them. Feet shuffled rapidly and dust flew around their faces.

"I've found it!" Mr. Waldly exclaimed. He pulled a large black oval shaped stone from his bag. It was etched with symbols - hieroglyphs to be exact. "I need to get near her," he said. "The stone will do the rest."

"What is it?" Charlie asked. "It's a Scarab. Rub it and speak the word OSIRIS and the Scarab will come to life and well... it's a rather nasty beetle... and has a penchant for anything enchanted... like itself.

"Why would you carry that around in your bag Mr. Waldly?!" Charlie said. "For times like these my dear. One never knows when one is going to run into an evil witch!"

"How do you propose getting near her?" Charlie enquired. "Well, I'm not sure about that part..." Mr. Waldly replied.

Before Mr. Waldly had the opportunity to continue, Charlie had snatched the stone from Mr. Waldly and crawled between the legs of the guards and the Shahzadeh.

She darted towards the Wiccan at breakneck speed leaping onto the boulders from the ground and jumping from one to the next. Her trail shoes were perfect for the terrain and within seconds she found herself standing under the Wiccan who looked down

131

at her surprised by her guile.

"You've come to me my dear... how delightful. You are a beautiful thing," the Wiccan said in a lascivious tone.

The Wiccan descended to the ground slowly. When she was close enough Charlie opened her hand and spoke the word OSIRIS at the top of her voice.

Nothing happened. "OSIRIS," she said again. Again, nothing happened.

The Wiccan looked on in amusement.

"Damn it," Charlie thought. "I need to rub it!" She reached for the stone and made the faintest of contact with her index finger as the Wiccan grabbed her by both wrists and squeezed very tightly, digging her long nails deep into Charlie's arms. They ran with blood and Charlie screamed.

Charlie had stamina and strength in buckets. In her screams she flicked her index finger across the opal and mouthed the word "OSIRIS".

The black opal immediately shimmered blue and green and grew. It buzzed as it grew larger and larger. In a second its surface split open to reveal legs, eyes, and a jaw.

It launched itself onto the Wiccan and clamped its jaw against her chest and its legs around her body. The Wiccan staggered backwards and released Charlie from her grip. Charlie stumbled backwards and fell from the boulder, twenty feet above the ground onto the rocks below.

Mr. Waldly had risen to his feet and looked on helplessly with the Shahzadeh and her guards as Charlie fell to the ground.

Time seemed to slow down.

And then on the rocks below appeared Charlie's Emissary who caught and clasped Charlie in her hands. Then, in an instant, both vanished.

The Shahzadeh and her guards dashed forward to tackle the Wiccan but, as they rounded the boulders, there was a flash of light and all that remained were the charred remains of the scarab.

"Who was that?" asked the Shahzadeh.

"Charlie's Emissary." replied Mr. Waldly. "She is safe now."

CHAPTER 27

Miss Tweedie

Charlie and the Emissary Levante reappeared on a narrow street lined with Chestnut trees.

It was early morning.

The birds were chirping, and a milk carriage trundled down the street. The milk bottles let out a familiar and reassuring rattling sound as the carriage ran over bumps in the road.

Charlie steadied herself. She was becoming accustomed to the shock of translocation. She glanced across the road to the name plate fixed to a red brick wall. It read 'Wickles Way N20´. We're back in London, she thought.

"Follow me," Emissary Levante said. "They won't be far behind. It was too dangerous to meet your Custodian over there in the mountains but there is another nearby. She will have what you need.

"Who... or what isn't far behind?" Charlie asked. She prompted herself on the latter as she had already encountered the Unremembered and the Wiccan and was fully prepared for anything but the ordinary.

"Here we are," said Levante.

They stood before a typical 1950's London suburban house. Number Six.

Net curtains hung in the bay window. The metal gate squeaked as it swung open. The curtains fluttered as the face of an elderly lady peered through the glass. She smiled at the visitors and closed the curtains before making her way slowly to the front door.

Levante and Charlie stood for at least a couple of minutes as locks turned and latches were unfastened.

Finally, the door opened and there stood Miss Tweedie. She was 85 and stood at 5 feet and 2 inches. Her hair was short and brilliant white with tightly knit curls. She wore a beige woollen cardigan and brown woollen skirt below the knee and flower-patterned slippers. Her eyes were small and hazelnut but exuded kindness - to the point of being hypnotic.

"Well, come in my dears," Miss Tweedie said. We wouldn't want them spotting you would we now?"

Charlie entered first and Levante followed having to duck as she passed through the doorway.

"Come into the lounge," Miss Tweedie said. "You look like you could do with a nice cup of tea and biscuits. I'll put the kettle on and you can put your feet up and relax my loves."

The room was perfectly ordered. Photos hung in frames. There must have been over a hundred covering every inch of the walls. Lace cloths covered the backs of the chairs, sofa, and side tables.

Charlie wandered the room looking at the photos. They were ordered according to dates handwritten on the corners. They were all black and white. Charlie realised that Miss Tweedie appeared in all of them but there was something very odd. She looked the same as she did before she left the lounge to make tea.

As though she had never been young.

Levante sat in one of the chairs and crossed her legs.

"You can't sit there," someone said. "That's my mistress' chair."

"No, you can't sit there. You'll have to move", another voice said.

Levante looked up and saw two budgerigars perched in a large bird cage. Levante moved over to another chair quietly.

"Well done, that's it. Here she comes," the birds chirped.

Miss Tweedie came back into the room carrying a tray with a teapot and three cups and saucers and a platter of biscuits - jammy dodgers, custard creams, chocolate digestives, pink wafers and bourbons.

The teapot reminded her of her time in the home of the Shahzadeh and the ensuing events with the Wiccan.

"My, my, you have had a wild few days," Miss Tweedie said. "You've travelled across the world and back. That encounter in the mountains with the Wiccan must have been terrifying my lovely."

"But how do you know? I didn't say anything," said Charlie.

"No, but you thought it my dear and well I hear those thoughts," replied Miss Tweedie.

Levante spoke up. "We must move quickly. Charlie could not make it to her first Custodian."

"Yes, yes, all in good time," Mrs Tweedie said as she poured the tea. "There's sugar if you want it and biscuits of course. Do tuck in."

"Miss Tweedie," Charlie enquired. "How is it you appear the same in all those photos?"

"You do have a keen eye!" Miss Tweedie exclaimed. "It's a long story my dear but let's just say I've been around for a good few years."

"Long story, ooh we know, we know!" chirped the budgerigars.

"Oh, do pipe down!" said Miss Tweedie. "She wasn't asking you!"

Through the net curtains Miss Tweedie could see the sky beginning to turn from clear blue to overcast as the heavens opened.

"Mmmm… maybe we should hurry along," said Miss Tweedie." What I have for you isn't in the house. It's in the garden… well off the garden more precisely. Follow me if you would?"

"Ooh we know, we know what's in the garden. You're one of them… aren't you? A new Emissary? We know what's waiting for you… we know, we know!" chirped the budgerigars.

Mrs Tweedie tutted as they all left the room and went through the kitchen to the back garden.

They emerged into the most beautifully kept garden with enormous hedges all around mixed in with azaleas, peonies and hydrangeas and a cluster of blossom trees at the back. A pristine lawn covered the ground surrounded by a path of small round flagstones. In the middle of the lawn stood a tall square wooden post with signs in the shape of arrows pointing outward from all four sides.

Miss Tweedie pointed to the signs. "Choose one," she said.

Charlie walked closer to the post to read what was written on the signs.

'Blessed' pointed north, 'Lucky' pointed west and 'True' pointed east. Charlie turned back towards the house and Miss Tweedie and Levante. The last sign pointed south towards her, Miss Tweedie, Levante and the house. On the sign was written… nothing. It was blank.

"I choose south," Charlie spoke confidently.

"Oh, that's a good choice my dear," replied Miss Tweedie. "Away we go!"

CHAPTER 28

The Child

The child awoke shivering and frightened in its solitude. It couldn't hear anything even when its lungs were bursting from its roaring bellow.

It awoke as it had thousands of times before - in the darkness of its home buried deep below the valley of the Wretched.

It did not know its origin. All it knew was its home and the valley above it. Its home to be exact was a network of tunnels and Chambers which ran for several miles. They had been constructed many years before the child was born.

The construction had been clearly planned to create a self-sustainable environment. It was built around a subterranean spring and at its heart was a plentiful garden of vegetables, herbs, shrubs and flowers which drew its light from hundreds of fine holes burrowed in the valley bed.

The Chambers were lined with stone and along the walls of each Chamber was carved the head of a beast (different for each Chamber).

Natural gases permeated the Chambers at marked intervals along the walls allowing lighting and heating through open flames which emitted from large stone spouts protruding from the walls.

He could hear the thud of the army of the Wretched marching

above him. Never had he heard so many of them. He wanted to see more and made his way steadily upward through the Chambers until he reached an opening in the hillside. He had never left the Chambers. They had been his home for as long as he could remember, and he rarely ventured to the surface as he was doing now.

He was naked. There had never been any reason to cover himself as far as he could recall and therefore, he never contemplated doing so. In any event, he did not possess any clothes.

The underground stream served as his bath. It was naturally heated and was most pleasurable to use. Consequently, the child was very clean. His hair was brown and extremely long. Occasionally, the child cut it roughly with a blade he had fashioned from the granite which lay strewn about the Chambers floors. The child wore it in a bun and secured it with a twig taken from a tree root.

The child peered out through the hillside opening and couldn't believe his eyes.

Thousands upon thousands of Wretched were marching through the valley accompanied by a variety of beasts the largest of which were immense mammoth like creatures pulling huge wooden slings. Hundreds of rabid dogs ran in front and behind, occasionally being trampled by the mammoths. The child could hear chanting,

"Death to the Emissaries, death to the order of the Society, death, death, death! All hail the Wiccan!"

It was a sight to behold. The grotesque forms of the Wretched - tall, short, emaciated, bulging, hunched, twisted and all filthy and boil ridden. All were waving weapons of different shapes and sizes - clubs, daggers, sabres, swords, lances, pikes and axes.

These were unsophisticated warriors with little or no training but their number and insatiable and unrelenting desire for killing made them irrepressible.

They advanced rapidly and the ground beneath them shuddered with every step.

The child looked on in amazement.

He had never seen a Wretched. They were very different from his more regular form. The child wasn't at all scared. He was more curious than anything else.

He wanted to reach out and touch them. Their skin was boiled, viscous and hirsute. Their feet and hands were oversized by comparison to the rest of their bodies and heads. Their toes and fingers were hooked and barbed like talons. Their teeth were sparse, long and jagged and their eyes were black and moved left to right in rapid bug-like fashion.

He waited patiently as the masses passed overhead until the stragglers stumbled forward from the rear and there were no more. He couldn't help himself escape the desire to follow. Never had he ventured from his home before as he emerged from the ground into the valley above him.

The child stood motionless with his eyes closed taking in the smell and sound of his surroundings. He could sense everything pulsating around and under him - the ground and air, the flora and fauna. He could sense every part of his naked body both inside and out.

He never had these sensations below ground. His exposure to the elements had triggered something inside of him and the feeling was intense and overpowering for a short while.

A thunderous noise grew ever louder in his head and the universe spun uncontrollably in his mind's eye. All at once, the noise stopped and everything in his universe converged into a single cell which shrunk to microscopic size until finally it vanished and all that was left was silence and a white infinity. He opened his eyes.

Looking ahead of him he could see the Wretched and behind him he tuned his ears into the pattering of feet and the low tone of menacing growls.

The sun was setting, and it reflected off dozens of eyes which were advancing rapidly towards the child. A pack of wolves had detected his sweeter smell to that of the Wretched. The wolves encircled the boy prowling, growling, yapping, and awaiting their leader's sign to pounce. They desperately resisted the ferrel urge to tear into his skin and rip him to pieces.

The male and female alphas edged forward as the boy stood motionless and quiet with his eyes shut. Then the alphas pounced as the others immediately followed.

Instantly, the child opened his eyes, and the wolves froze and hung mid-flight. The child turned his head this way and that, admiring the wolves' agility as they remained stuck in the air. He passed through them stroking their backs and scratching their necks. All at once, he blinked, and they fell to the ground. They picked themselves up and sat back on their haunches bowing their heads in deference. The child owned them now and they would do as he commanded.

The child turned and walked forward to pursue the Wretched hoard and the wolves obediently followed.

CHAPTER 29

Quinque Unus

Alexander, Father Raherius and Grecale and Ostro stood motionless. There was nothing they could have done. Stephen was lost and they had to keep moving to survive.

"Down into the catacombs! We need to make up time, yes, we need to make up time! That's it! Make it up! Not recover lost time... well actually... yes, that's exactly what we need to do! Recover lost time by making it up! You see... that's clear... isn't it? Of course, it is!... that's how we save Stephen. No time to lose!... well maybe there is time to lose... hee hee!... oh, it's all very complicated. We need to join the others!"

"Who?" Alexander enquired.

Grecale and Ostro stood by and nodded at Father Raherius.

"The others, my boy. The others like you. You're not the only one you know. There are others. Eight to be precise. But I don't know if they've all been revealed. We must travel to see an old friend... the Archduke... and I know just how to get there.

Father Raherius shuffled down the corridor as the voices of the cathedral choir echoed overhead. Quick step, all of you! Grecale and Ostro ducked their heads in the usual manner to fit through the corridors as they became narrower and lower the further they walked. But to Alexander it seems like they were walking in circles. Every minute or so they would pass the same ossuary of priests long since passed.

"Hang on," said Alexander who was struggling to fit through the corridor himself. "We've been walking in circles for ten minutes now. We don't seem to be going anywhere. And this corridor seems to be shrinking

"Hee hee… ten minutes my boy… are you sure? Sure, are you? I think it's been more like ten hours. Yes, ten hours… Time gets a little fragmented down here…"

Alexander looked behind him to see Grecale and Ostro crawling along the floor of the corridor and when he turned back towards Father Raherius he found that he himself was also crawling.

It was becoming very difficult to breath now as the walls and ceiling of the corridor closed in around them.

"We're almost there!" declared Father Raherius. "Just around this bend… there we are."

Alexander could barely move now and his vision became very blurred as he heard a knock and the creaking of a hatch door opening as a hand reached in to pull out Father Raherius. And with that Alexander promptly passed out.

He awoke in a soft velvet armchair in a semi-lit room next to an open fire. Something with a large raspy tongue was licking the side of his face and something else was butting and rubbing itself against his legs. As his eyes opened, his heart jumped as he made out the shapes of two very big cats staring at him millimetres from his face.

"Il est réveillé!" a voice shouted. "Merveilleux!"

"Worry not, mon cher! The cats are your friends. This is Freya and Skadi. They belong to Tom and Zoe now. Your cat will be here soon. They are never far away from their Emissaries.

"Allow me to introduce myself. I am Archduke Guillaume de Lorraine and this is my most humble abode."

"Where are we?" Alexander enquired.

"En France bien sûr! Au domaine de La Lorraine." the Archduke replied.

"France but that's impossible. We were in London…"

"Ah mon ami… you must have learnt by now that strange things can happen, non?"

The large metal knob turned on the sitting room door and Father Raherius shuffled in, followed by Grecale and Ostro. Then the very imposing figures of Tramontane and Maestro. Behind them followed Tom.

"This is sooo exciting… sooo exciting! I am sooo excited, thrilled. Yes, absolutely thrilled!" Father Raherius declared exuberantly.

He could hardly contain himself as he performed a little jig around the room.

"Alexander, you remember Tom from the Sanctuary?" said the Archduke. Zoe is upstairs resting."

"Where's Stephen?" Tom enquired.

"Taken by the Wiccan," Father Raherius answered. "But we will get him back… mark my words… mark my words… we will… we will. But first we must wait for the other…"

"The other?" Tom asked.

"The other one of you. That will make four... well five with Stephen. More than half of you!... this is sooo exciting!"

"Let's put on some dinner, shall we?" said the Archduke calmly. Whilst we wait for the other one. She has a name you know, Father Raherius."

Father Raherius was in his own world dancing around the room but not entirely absent to have heard the Archduke afford him the opportunity to announce the other one's name.

"Ah yes, yes, yes... her name... Charlotte. Well, Charlie. Yes, Charlie, Charlie, Charlie... she's been with Mr. Waldly. I think you are all going to get along merrily..."

And with that, there was a loud knock at the front door.

"Les voilà!" declared the Archduke as he moved into the entrance hall.

He opened the door as he announced "Mr Waldly, it's been a very long time..."

"Mr. Waldly has been held up my dear... I am Miss Tweedie. We found these two adorable felines just outside the cemetery."

Parvati (an Asiatic Lioness) and Li Shou (a Chinese Snow Leopard) slipped around Miss Tweedie gently and ambled to the open fire.

"Miss Tweedie, your reputation precedes you! Quel plaisir! Bienvenue!"

Skadi had awoken and joined Freya downstairs sensing Parvati and Li Shou's arrival. It was quite the sight to behold - a Tiger,

Jaguar, Lioness and Leopard together in one room. These cats came from an ancient ancestral line and were much bigger than their contemporary kin. They wove in and out of each other as if performing a ritual dance and the flames of the fire and lighting in the room grew momentarily. Then they settled on the floor as the other guests entered the room.

Zoe had come downstairs after Skadi.

Charlie entered after Miss Tweedie. She turned to Tom, Zoe and Alexander, instantly sensing they were like her.

"Hello," she said. "I'm Charlie. I'm not sure what's going on. It's been a very strange few days, but my mother has told me to bear with it. Maybe we could talk?"

"That would be great Charlie," replied Tom. "I think we might have a lot in common. Alexander, Zoe, shall we sit next door?"

The group filed into the library leaving the Emissaries, Father Raherius, the Archduke and Miss Tweedie in the sitting room.

The cats stood and followed the group into the library as Tom closed the door and the Archduke looked on smiling.

The group gathered around the large table at the centre of the room. The Compendium of Alchemists' Abstruse Contrivances lay on the table and Alexander recognised it instantly.

"That is the book I left behind at Oxford with Miss Jones." Alexander stated.

"It's the second edition. The one you found in Oxford was the first edition." replied Tom. "I assume they are the same but I'm not sure. What I do know is they are the only two in existence."

"Compendium of Alchemists' Abstruse Contrivances - that's a very peculiar title." Charlie interjected. "Oh, sorry. Where are my manners? I'm Charlie, pleased to meet you all."

"I'm Tom."

"I'm Zoe."

"I'm Alexander."

"What are we all doing here?" Charlie enquired.

"That's a very good question!" Zoe exclaimed.

"Tom and I have also had a very strange couple of days!"

"You can say that again!" Tom affirmed.

"Me too!" said Alexander.

"Me too!" said Charlie.

The Great Cats circled the group purring loudly.

Skadi took her position next to Zoe and Freya took her position next to Tom. Parvati took her position next to Alexander and Li Shou took her position next to Charlie.

They each rubbed their heads fondly against their respective charges and were petted in return.

The synergy between the cats and the group was unprecedented. The air filled with endorphins and the group felt euphoric. They instinctively joined hands as the table in the room began to rise from the floor along with the group. The cats looked up from the floor below as the compendium rose above the table with the group.

Tom parted from the group and moved into the middle of what was now a circle positioned above the table and the compendium.

A current of energy ran out of Tom and into Zoe, Alexander and Charlie.

He was transfixed, unable to move but his eyes were wide open and saw everything in space and time and the worlds in between.

Zoe, Alexander and Charlie began to grow as their clothes stretched and tore with the transformation.

Tom lifted his hand, and the curtains were pulled from the windows and flew across the room wrapping themselves around the others.

The winds howled outside as the windows broke open. The pages of the compendium turned forwards and backwards.

Those outside the room knew they could not enter for fear of interfering in the group's energy and risking their lives during the transformation.

The cats looked on undeterred. They and their ancestors had witnessed the transformation several times over.

The night sky exploded around the Archduke's residence with thunder and lightning until two bolts struck the home and gradually worked their way over the roof and down the brickwork seeking out an aperture.

Eventually, the bolts of lightning found the opened windows and the group. The bolts stopped edging forwards and crackled as if they were consciously watching and waiting for the perfect moment to strike. For a few seconds the clocks in the room stopped, the winds stopped, everything stopped including the group and the compendium. Everything became motionless and silent.

Then one last page turned in the compendium to reveal a double-page stencil. In the top hand corner of each page pointing down was a single lightning bolt. Running across the bottom of the pages were eight human figures. Above the figures were objects - two pendants, two rings, two bracelets and two brooches. Each housed an amulet.

Inscribed at the top middle of the left-hand page was the word 'Octo' and at the top middle of the right-hand page 'Unus'. Together they translated from Latin as 'One in Eight'.

Outside the room, Father Raherius led a chant. He, the Archduke, Miss Tweedie and the Emissaries all spoke the words "Octo Unus" in perfect unison gradually building in volume.

Of course, they were not eight in the Archduke's home. They were four. Poor Stephen had been taken by the Wiccan and the remainder had yet to reveal themselves. Nevertheless, their energy was so great now that they could all see each other across the space and time which divided them.

Suddenly, the lighting and thunder stopped as instantly as it had started, and the windows shut.

The chanting stopped.

The compendium descended slowly and settled on the table.

But the group remained suspended in the air with their eyes closed.

The Archduke, Father Raherius rose from their chairs; and Tramontane, Maestro, Grecale, Ostro and Levante did the same. They moved towards the door of the library. The Archduke turned the handle and pushed the door ajar slowly. The group were still suspended in the air. The cats looked on purring loudly. Tom opened his eyes and nodded at the Archduke.

"It's time," he said. "We must save Stephen... and there is another... a child... he is special..." With that, Tom closed his eyes and the lights began to flicker on and off in the room until the group had vanished and so had the cats.

Miss Tweedie stayed seated. She had turned to her knitting. She knew what was to come and there was nothing she could do to influence it.

Part 4

Henry

CHAPTER 30

Deliverance

The group and the cats reappeared in the hubbub of rush hour of the concourse at Waterloo Station. The worst place for them to be.

They were invisible to the human eye and without solid form so that the crowds passed through them in large numbers. The cats were used to the sensation but all apart from Charlie (who herself struggled) had never experienced this before and it was extremely unpleasant.

They all stooped and fell to the ground overwhelmed by the trauma it caused. The cats stood by them knowing they would adapt. They had seen this many times before. The group instinctively clasped the cats' large necks and hoisted themselves from the ground as the cats led them through the crowds and onto one of the platforms.

The group took time to compose themselves. Then Alexander said, "There's Stephen! He's boarding that train."

"Stephen!" Alexander shouted. But Stephen had already boarded as the platform guard blew her whistle and the train began to roll out of the station.

"Quick," Tom said. "Everyone, get on!"

Zoe had already begun to dart forward but Skadi pulled her back. The others had already closed their eyes, imagined themselves aboard and disappeared and reappeared on the train.

"Oh," Zoe said. "Ok then. It better not be like this all the time. It's too easy!" She closed her eyes with Skadi and both reappeared on the train with the rest.

The group and the cats were making their way through the train searching for Stephen. Eventually, they reached the carriage in which Stephen was located. Stephen was joking and laughing in a group of young professionals.

"This is the past." Tom stated. "That is Stephen several days ago before he transformed. Something happened here which created a connection with the Unremembered. We need to wait and observe."

The group and the cats found themselves spaces about the carriage and then watched.

Several stops passed by until Stephen fell to sleep and that was when it happened.

The sky turned dark and the carriage became extremely cold. The passengers vanished one-by-one and the train gradually changed into a much older steam-driven model with wooden panelling, velvet drapes across the windows and brass candle lit lanterns.

Stephen awoke and looked understandably confused.

The group looked on as he rose from his seat and edged toward the front of the carriage looking around him in bemusement as the train pulled into the station and came to a stop.

He reached the end of the carriage and that was when the group saw the Unremembered through the glass panel of the carriage door. Charlie shuddered. She had seen them before and more importantly they had seen her.

This time was different. The Unremembered didn't enter the carriage. They stood quietly but Charlie could hear their children sobbing.

The cats growled.

Tom closed his eyes and tried to connect with Stephen. That is Stephen of the past. But it didn't work. Then Tom realised… there was no past, present or indeed future… only now… whenever that was.

Stephen opened the carriage door, unaware of the Unremembered behind it. The Unremembered recoiled and pressed themselves back. The group edged forwards cautiously as the cats followed and continued to growl.

Stephen looked down and standing on the platform was the same little man dressed in black who Charlie had encountered in the arcade and Stephen had encountered in the crypt at St. Paul's. He did not recoil. He stared at Stephen with those lifeless bloodshot eyes as before, turning and walking down the platform as he disappeared into the fog.

"This isn't where Stephen was taken," said Alexander. "He was taken in the crypt at St. Paul's."

"But this is where we will find him," said Tom." This is where he first encountered them."

Tom and the others descended from the train and saw Stephen's silhouette ahead of them by the exit. He had paused in front of a door.

They hurried down the platform shouting instinctively, "Stephen, stop! Don't go in there!" But, of course, he couldn't hear them as he stepped into the waiting room and the door slammed shut behind him. This time, his Emissary was nowhere to be seen. The circumstances had changed, and the Wiccan lay waiting.

The group edged towards the door.

The cats continued to growl, and sensing a presence behind them, turned to see the little man and a group of the Unremembered - men, women and children emerging from the wall lining the platform. The cats growled furiously as the little man hissed back and advanced with the group.

Then, a further gathering of the Unremembered appeared blocking the platform ahead of them. This only left the waiting room and the exit as a means of escape.

The group knew they were trapped and being pushed towards the doorway to the waiting room through which Stephen had disappeared.

Zoe moved forward to look out beyond the exit and found herself looking back at herself as if she were looking into a mirror.

The cats took their positions on each side of the group. Skadi and Freya on one side and Parvati and Li Shou on the other.

They began clawing the ground generating an ultra highpitched screech which reverberated all around. The group only heard it momentarily after which it became muted to them. However, for the Unremembered it was excruciatingly painful.

The cats and the group were outside of their dimension and inside that of the Unremembered. The cats instinctively knew that this was the only way they could repel the Unremembered.

Their ghostly apparitions held their hands to their ears as they tried to battle against the noise. But the cats clawed ever more intensely until it was too much for the Unremembered to bear. They retreated shaking their heads violently from side to side in a very inhuman manner.

Tom stood by the door in front of the others. He had closed his eyes trying to sense what was behind the door but saw nothing.

He turned to the others. "Prepare yourselves," he said. "Somewhere behind this door is Stephen but I cannot see what else."

Tom turned the doorknob and pushed the door ajar. He stepped through the doorway first as Zoe, then Charlie and finally Alexander followed. The door slammed shut as the cats remained on the platform prowling back and forth.

The moment they entered the waiting room they all experienced the same feeling of falling in a spiral pattern. It was as if they were on a fairground helter-skelter. It was pitch black and they shouted to each other but could only hear the echo of their own voice. They continued to fall for what seemed an age until finally they stopped. They couldn't feel their feet on solid ground. They continued to shout to each other, hearing only the echo of their own voice and all around them it remained pitch-black.

Then each of them heard another voice.

"Well, well. You all decided to join me. What a wonderful surprise! You've made matters so much simpler. Your fates are inevitable, of course, as is that of the pitiful humankind!"

Each of the group could hear her breathing and smell her as she drew closer to each of them, Then, they felt the Wiccan as she drew the talon-like nail of her index finger across each of their cheeks.

Their hearts pounded heavily but their resolve was unwavering. They had communed in the library of the Archduke and realised then that they needed only to mask their surroundings and focus on one another to create a telepathic bond.

Tom, Zoe, Charlie and Alexander closed their eyes and the Wiccan's voice became instantly muffled. The Wiccan felt their unity growing in strength as Stephen was awoken in his cell to join his fellow Emissaries telepathically.

The Wiccan knew that the only way to break their connection was to strike a fatal blow upon one of the group. She had wanted more time to torture and break each of them, but they were much more powerful than she had anticipated and this left her no choice. She drew the ancient blade used to end Madame Vauqelin's life and reappeared floating above Stephen in his cell.

Stephen was pinned face down to the floor by chains which wove around and criss crossed his body. He was extremely fatigued, weak and without his ring which the Wiccan had somehow managed to remove when she captured him.

The others could visualise the cell and saw the Wiccan floating above Stephen as she aimed the dagger at the nape of his neck just below his skull.

The children concentrated like never before as their amulets began to shine evermore brightly until they found themselves reunited and holding hands.

The Wiccan dove towards Stephen with the blade extended ahead of her but as she did so the ring in her pocket burned so brightly that it scolded the Wiccan's thigh and blinded her as it tumbled from her pocket to the ground. The Wiccan continued her descent all the same and struck Stephen penetrating his skin and cartilage. She drove the blade into him as he screamed in pain.

But her aim had faltered owing to the scolding and bright light of the ring. She had struck Stephen on his shoulder. She had not noticed that Stephen had found the strength to reach for the ring which had fallen just next to his left hand and place it on the index of his right hand where it belonged.

The others were in a total meditative state. Their eyes were now open and pure white.

Stephen felt a jolt of energy run through his body as his eyes also turned pure white. He twisted his body upward snapping the metal chains like paper.

The Wiccan had no time to remove the dagger as she was thrown back by the force of Stephen's sudden movement. The hilt and pommel of the dagger twisted against the floor as Stephen turned pushing the blade sideways and out through Stephen's arm.

Blood ran thickly from the wound but did not deter Stephen. Pointing his index finger and ring towards the Wiccan he summoned the power of the north-east wind and thrust the Wiccan upwards. The wind's force was too great for the Wiccan as she was tossed and turned. She fought and shrieked until eventually she could no longer be heard and there was silence.

Stephen picked himself up from the ground, grabbing the dagger as he rose. He placed it in his belt. As he looked up, he was no longer in the cell but standing among the others between Tom and Zoe.

Tom reached out his hand and found the doorknob to the waiting room. He opened the door and one by one the group stepped out onto the platform. Tom, Stephen, Zoe, Charlie and Alexander.

The Unremembered were nowhere to be seen. Only the little man remained at the far end of the platform staring angrily through his bloodshot eyes at the group.

The group were greeted warmly by the cats who had been standing guard by the door.

Stephen collapsed onto the platform. He had lost a lot of blood from the injury to his shoulder.

The cats knew immediately what they had to do. Very carefully, they lay down next to Stephen and gently rubbed their heads against his body as they purred in unison. The cats began emitting multi-coloured sparkles which sunk into Stephen. Gradually, Stephen regained some colour in his face and the wound on his arm began to heal until all that was left was a small scar.

The group turned to the exit and like Zoe earlier found themselves looking back at themselves as if they were looking through a mirror.

"I'm not sure how we leave this place?" said Tom.

The group heard cackled laughter from the end of the platform. It was the little man.

Then Stephen remembered that Grecale had taken him from the station to the Sanctuary days before. How had he done it?

Stephen turned to the others. "I need to retrace my steps with

Grecale when he rescued me. I think it's the only way we can leave. Form a chain with the cats and when I reach out for you take my hand."

The group followed Stephen's instructions, and each held their cat - Tom with Freya; Zoe with Skadi; Charlie with Li Shou and Alexander with Parvati forming a link with one another.

Stephen closed his eyes and slowly through the clouded memories of his mind found himself back with Grecale the moment they left the waiting room. Just as Grecale was about to transition, Stephen reached out to the others. Tom grabbed Stephen's hand and in an instant they all vanished from the platform.

CHAPTER 31

The Transference

The group re-emerged at the Sanctuary.

It was not the idyllic place where they had met Madame Vauqelin only a few days before but a ruin.

Of course, Charlie had never been here before but was immediately aware of its importance to the group and emotionally moved by the devastation. A tear ran down her cheek.

Tom, Zoe, Stephen and Alexander had been rushed away quickly but now had time to take in their surroundings and recall their brief but seminal time here.

Tom led the group through the once heavenly gardens of Madame Vauqelin to the Chamber.

The great compass which made up the floor was no longer visible. The Cimmerian had burst through its center and rubble, glass and shard lay scattered across the Chamber.

Tom looked up to where the once beautiful dome had adorned the Society's home. It too had been destroyed in the attack.

Tom paused for a moment to recollect his memories when he first walked into the Chamber. He had looked up at the magnificent dome and seen the glistening sun casting its rays through a gold circumference in the middle of which sat a red stone. Of course, that circumference was the compass which had been projected onto the Chamber floor below.

In that moment, Tom realised the importance of that compass to the Society and its structure. It defined each of the Emissaries and now the group by their wind sign.

It had been the first artefact crafted for the Society at the time of its founding. The stone, for all the misfortune it brought, was also part of the compass.

Tom began searching for the compass and stone and asked the group to do the same.

"Everyone, look for a compass. It's about the size of a tennis ball and inset with a red stone. We must find it!"

In her haste to destroy the Sanctuary and end Madame Vauqelin's life, the Wiccan had overlooked the one object which brought meaning to the Society and was at the heart of its power.

The group hunted everywhere, as did the cats, but the compass was nowhere to be found in the Chamber. The group had not witnessed Madame Vauqelin drawing it to her hand and secreting in her pocket before the Wiccan had struck that fatal blow with her blade.

Freya, Skadi, Li Chou and Parvati moved towards the edge of the abyss. They sensed their brothers and sisters - the clowder which had sought Madame Vauqelin's body when she fell into the abyss.

The cats began to emerge from the abyss one by one until two of the largest emerged pulling the body of Madame Vauqelin gently behind them.

They brought her body forward and laid it to rest at the centre of the Chamber floor. Madame Vauqelin had been a small lady, but her lifeless body seemed so much smaller.

The cats instinctively rubbed themselves against her and some licked her hair. They purred in synchrony. The energy they created pulsated throughout the Chamber and a warm pink light filled the air. They were trying to revive Madame but despite the rejuvenating powers of the cats they could not stir Madame from the dead. She had been executed by the Wiccan with an enchanted dagger and death was absolute.

Tom stepped forward.

Tears streamed from his eyes and ran down his cheeks. He had only known Madame Vauqelin for a short while, but she had touched his heart and soul with her maternal kindness and wisdom. He knelt beside her body. His tears reacted with the illumination of the cats creating flashes of intense luminosity.

One flash shone through the fabric of her jacket and revealed a round shiny object in her pocket. Tom noticed and placed his hand gently in the pocket. He clasped the object and removed it slowly.

His tears stopped when he realised what the object was. It was the compass, and the red lodestone was inset at its centre.

"What is it?" Zoe enquired.

Tom rose and turned to the group who immediately recognised the object.

"It's the compass," Tom announced. "Now... now," He stuttered in anxiety. It had all come about so quickly but he understood what had to be done.

"We are ready to take this fight to the Wiccan. The Society is much more than this Chamber. It is the will and force in each of us. There are four more of us out there. We must find them before the Wiccan does. The Society has been reborn and today marks a new chapter in its story."

Tramontane, Maestro, Grecale, Ostro and Levante appeared in the Chamber and stepped forward. Each of them removed their hoods and cloaks. The group were shocked by their appearance. Their faces were pale and scared with centuries of battle. Their heads were shaven, and their deep yellow eyes were now completely revealed. The Emissaries were born human but had evolved physically over time to adapt to their surroundings.

"Why are your eyes permanently yellow?" enquired Zoe.

"It's to do with our blood. When we commune, it increases the blood circulation until eventually the eyes' pigmentation is permanently altered."

"And your skin is so pale." Zoe said.

"We were raised to keep our faces covered at all times. And so, they never saw daylight. But you are different. Madame never wanted your generation to hide from the world. She wanted you to abandon some of the old traditions. Not all, mind you. Some are there for good reason and will protect you from those dangerous elements that wish to do you harm."

"And the scars?" Zoe asked.

"Zoe, stop." Tom interjected.

"No, Tom it's fine." You need to know everything, and Zoe is the most curious one amongst you. Keep a balance on that curiosity of yours Zoe. It is both your strength and flaw." Tramontane warned.

Tramontane like the other old Emissaries knew of the group's destiny. They could see their futures in every detail. But, of course, they could never reveal them. And it was why they needed to now part ways. The old Emissaries could have no part to play in the group's future. They could not risk influencing their fate.

"We have been involved in many battles over the centuries and bear the scars of those battles. We are tired and old Father Time catches up on all of us. Now is your time. A time for you to pick up the mantle and carry it forward. You will not be alone. You know there are more of you out there. You sense it. Your brothers and sisters. They are with their Emissaries and Custodians and will join you soon in your new home. But for now, our work is done. You have each other and we must leave you.

"What?!" Zoe exclaimed. "You can't just suddenly leave us like that. We have only just started on this journey!"

"Zoe," Tom said quietly, firmly, and reassuringly in a single tone.

"You have many friends out there. Many of whom you are yet to meet. And the cats will look after you."

Skadi appeared by Zoe's side and bent her head forward to position it under Zoe's palm. Zoe instinctively dropped to the ground and grabbed Skadi's neck pulling Skadi tight against her... and cried.

"I'm afraid," she said in a muffled voice.

"We all are," Charlie said.

"But we have each other." Alexander said.

"We will always have each other." Stephen said.

Freya, Parvati and Li Shou appeared next to each of their ward.

"It is time," said Tramontane.

Old Emissaries Maestro, Grecale, Ostro and Levante stepped forward.

Tramontane approached Tom, Maestro approached Zoe, Grecale approached Stephen, Ostro approached Alexander and Levante approached Charlie.

The old Emissaries raised their hands and put them on the group's foreheads and closed their eyes.

This was known as the transference. All the experience and knowledge of the old Emissaries was passed to the group. Their knowledge had been passed to them by the second generation as had the first generation to the second.

For the group, the world spun in the Chamber as they felt the intake of information. They couldn't see or feel all of the past experiences they were absorbing. That would be too much. They felt the flow of energy fill their veins.

The feeling subsided and they opened their eyes. They looked around and found themselves alone with their cats.

The old Emissaries were gone. The other cats were gone. The body of Madame Vauqelin was gone.

Tom had been holding the compass and red lodestone in his

hand throughout the transference. This had never happened in the history of the Society. The lodestone amplified the transference in such a way that Tom imbued the knowledge of all the old Emissaries at once. He would learn over time that it was to make him a formidable force.

Tom turned to the others.

"There is a terrible reckoning coming. An army of the Wretched led by the Wiccan but there is also something far stronger. It is ancient. It took the life of a Custodian many years ago in London. His name was Henry. It took something very dear to the Society and has been lying in wait ever since. We need to travel to London with the compass and red lodestone and visit the place of Henry's passing."

They held hands instinctively to prepare for the transition. They realised that travelling was exhausting on their bodies but together it was a less strenuous endeavour.

CHAPTER 32

Bastet

It was a warm mid-Summer Sunday evening.

The light was beginning to turn, and a throng of people had descended on the palace grounds to join in the festivities of the street food fair.

Live Jamaican reggae resonated from the hilltop down the grounds below and the aromas of various culinary dishes wafting from the numerous marquees aligning the path around the palace filled the air.

Couples lay together and families played on the grass as dogs ran to and fro barking with excitement.

The group and the cats appeared under cover of a small thicket of chestnut trees at the foot of the hillside.

A young child stood in the clearing with a ball in his hands. He stared at the group. He had witnessed their arrival and his mouth was hanging open in amazement. Charlie winked at him and smiled. Her smile was warm and comforting, almost enchanting. The boy smiled back and waved at Charlie. She waved back. Then the child turned and skipped away. He threw the ball on the grass and resumed his kick around with his mate.

"It happened up by the concourse on the mezzanine." said Tom.

"I've seen pictures of this place before," said Alexander. "I mean,

I know it's Alexandra Palace. I've seen pictures of Alexandra Palace before. I've never been here. But I've seen pictures of the building in the Compendium. Not the version at the Duke's residence but the one I found at the Oxford University library."

"Why were you looking for that book?" Stephen enquired.

"I was waiting for someone to ask that," said Alexander. I am… er… was… goodness knows… an undergraduate at Oxford studying History. I was researching the rise and fall of royal dynasties across Europe and came across the story of a French scribe called Nicolas Flamel and his wife Perenelle. They both seem to have known a number of Royal families during the 14th century. They appear in hundreds of journals across the European continent. That's when I happened upon Perinnelle's book 'The Compendium of Alchemists' Abstruse Contrivances' and that's when I was attacked. But there are drawings of this place in that book. I'm not sure how that can be. How old is this building? The book was published following Perinelle's death in 1397."

"It was opened in 1873 to mark Queen Victoria's 54th birthday but burned down a couple of weeks' later. It reopened in 1875. It burned down again in 1980 and reopened in 1988," Tom said. "It has hosted a multitude of events over the years - exhibitions, concerts, theatre." Tom stopped speaking for a moment. "Sorry, it's one of my favourite spots. I love the place. I moved nearby recently. My school is not far away. It's where I met Zoe. It's very strange that we're back here of all places…"

"That's all great Tom but how is it that it appears in a book written 500 years before it was built!" Alexander interjected. "I mean, I'm no expert but surely it isn't typical of 14th century architecture?…"

"Why did Henry come here that night? What was he doing? What did he find here?" Stephen enquired.

"Well I don't know about you boys but Charlie and I aren't standing around here any longer. We're going up onto the concourse, grabbing something to eat and enjoying this sunshine!" Zoe declared. With that, she grabbed Charlie's hand and pulled her away from the group as she ran out from under the thicket. "I love reggae!"

Charlie giggled and both girls broke into laughter as they ran up the hill together. "Bye boys! Skadi, stay with the others." Zoe shouted from the distance.

Charlie turned and winked at Parvati. Their first true moment. Parvati gave a smile by closing her eyes and knelt forward purring.

"Zoe! We need to stay together!" Tom retorted but it was too late. The girls had already disappeared into the crowds leaving the boys to trudge up the hill after them.

Zoe and Charlie found an open area near the stage where the band was playing. Zoe held Charlie by both hands as they spun around together smiling and laughing. This was such a release. A welcomed rush of normality to make up for the bizarre events of the last few days.

"Are you peckish?" Zoe asked Charlie.

"I'm famished," Charlie replied.

"Right then. Let's go and find some food then." Zoe said.

"But I don't have any money," Charlie said.

"Don't worry about that," Zoe replied. "Watch and learn!"

Zoe led Charlie up to one of the food stands selling fish and chips.

As they stood in the queue, two men appeared from behind the columns of the Palm Court entrance.

They were quite remarkable if one had been paying attention to them but otherwise blended into the crowd given its size.

They both wore double-breasted suit jackets with oversized lapels and flared trousers. On their feet, they wore platform leather shoes with rounded toes. One of the men stood no higher than four and a half feet (with the platforms). The other was at least six and a half feet. The smaller man wore glasses and his thin straight hair dyed black was plastered to his head with an excessive amount of grease. The taller man also wore glasses and had curly grey hair which hung around his head like a fluffy ball of cotton wool.

They moved towards the girls at pace and as they drew close the smaller man moved to one side, so he came up behind Charlie and the taller man behind Zoe. They both drew flick knives from their pockets and opened them ready to strike.

Zoe was chatting to two boys in the queue in front of them and paying no attention to her surroundings. Charlie, on the other hand, wasn't interested in the boys. She certainly wasn't as bold or flirtatious as Zoe. In this instance, it would save them both.

She had become used to people following her given her experience with Mr. Waldly in Covent Garden and her senses had become heightened following her transformation.

She swivelled rapidly on the balls of her feet and instinctively clapped her hands together. The two men had come so close but not close enough. They were catapulted backwards against the palace wall by the resonance of the clap.

Zoe launched towards the two men, but Charlie grabbed her arm and yanked her back.

"Not here Zoe," Charlie said firmly but in a hushed tone. "We mustn't draw attention to ourselves. We need to be discreet."

Zoe glared furiously at the men who were picking themselves off the ground. They glared back in defiance and would have been wiser not to do so. Zoe stared deep into their eyes and felt a fury building up inside of her. She turned her head to the side ever so slightly and small drops of blood rolled out from the men's noses. They knew it was time to leave and scarpered into the crowds.

"What was that?" Charlie asked.

"What was what?" Zoe replied.

"You know... you made their noses bleed... how, why did you do that?"

"I don't know. They were trying to hurt us. They deserved it! I shouldn't have stopped there! Anyway, how did you do that clapping thing?"

"I'm not sure. It just happened, I guess. It felt natural."

"Well, there you go. That's how it felt with me." Zoe was still fuming with the attack and more so that she had been caught unaware.

They both felt the soft fur coats of Skadi and Parvati against them. The cats had followed the boys up the hill to the palace.

"No one can see the cats, but people move around them to avoid walking into them... it's very odd," Stephen said.

"Oh, and by the way, we loved the spectacle," Alexander said wryly. "You clearly didn't need us."

"Are you both OK?" said Tom

"We're fine!" Zoe retorted brusquely.

Tom gave Zoe a concerned and caring look. He could clearly see she had been rattled and a fire was still raging inside her. Tom had a special bond with Zoe. He knew how complex she was and had witnessed the anger in her nature outside their school when she dispatched the bullies with such passion. Tom would need to keep that side of her nature in check. It would make her a formidable warrior, but Tom recognised that she may one day become a danger to herself and the group.

Suddenly, Tom was seeing through Henry's eyes and could hear the heaviness of his breathing as Henry scrambled onto the mezzanine hunting for markings on the mezzanine wall. Henry's breath froze in the night air.

Tom pointed up to the mezzanine. "That's where Henry met his end. He was searching for something very important to the Society. But it was night time."

"Let's go inside. There must be an internal staircase to take us up there." Alexander said.

The Palm Court annex had been recently renovated, and inside, away from the hubbub of the concourse, was an exhibition of the history of the palace.

Film and visual displays filled the court all telling stories of key events in the building's history.

As the group passed through the court, Charlie caught sight of a familiar face in one of the displays of people celebrating the opening of the palace on 24th May 1873.

There she was - Miss Tweedie dressed in a beautiful white lace gown with silk gloves and parasol surrounded by an entourage.

Charlie moved on to the next display. It told the story of the fire which destroyed the palace sixteen days later and its rebuilding. Lone and behold there was Miss Tweedie cutting the ribbon on 1st May 1875

And so Charlie moved on again and again each time seeing Miss Tweedie at the various events: Dr Holden's Magical Entertainment; The Venetian Fête (1880) ; Dr Barton's Airship (1888); Queen Mary's Visit (1888); Horse Racing (1896); Colney Cody's Wild West Show (1897); Edwardian Daredevil Zoe Shepard (1906); Percy Honri's New Pavillon (1910); the refugee and internment camps of WW1 and WW2; the BBC studio (1936); the concerts: Pink Floyd (1967); The Who (1969); Black Sabbath (1973); Grateful Dead (1974) and Queen (1979) until she came to the second fire on 10th July 1980.

Charlie had seen the photos in Miss Tweedie's sitting room and knew that Miss Tweedie had lived through several decades unchanged in her appearance. Nonetheless, when she saw Miss Tweedie again inspecting the damage to the Great Hall over hundred years since the palace was first built, she knew that the Society (and particularly Miss Tweedie) had a very special connection with this building.

"Charlie!" Alexander shouted from across the court. He beckoned her to follow them.

Charlie took one last look at Miss Tweedie inspecting the ruins in the Great Hall. She was looking at the rear wall where the famous Henry Willis organ once stood.

"Charlie!" Alexander shouted again.

"I'm coming," Charlie replied as she turned and headed across the court beyond the displays and the palms to the group. In the corner, hidden behind the entrance to the Phoenix pub was a locked door.

Stephen had forced it open as the others stood watch to make sure he was not spotted by staff. It was so busy and loud by the pub entrance no one would have noticed anyway.

When the coast was clear, the group slipped through the doorway one by one. Charlie went through and Alexander was the last as he closed the door behind him.

The doorway led to a system of subterranean passageways which wove themselves under the palace building. The passageways hadn't been used in decades and the vestiges of various events over the years were strewn across them wedged in corners and propped up against the stained bare brick walls. The air was stale and musty and the dripping of water could be heard everywhere. Rats scurried about looking for food.

There was a tunnel behind them which must have led to the rear entrance by the railway station. Ahead of them was a short stretch of about ten metres which the group took. At the end were steps which probably led down to grounds below the palace. To their right was a tunnel which probably led to the park and beyond. To their left was another tunnel that ran under the Great Hall and aligned the front of the palace. That was the direction the group needed to take to reach the mezzanine.

"This way!" Zoe exclaimed. She was still reeling from her and Charlie's encounter with the two assassins and was struggling to contain her pent-up anger. She moved to the front of the group.

"Can you hear that?" Stephen asked.

"What?" Tom replied.

"Silence," Stephen answered. "I can't hear the noises of the people above us on the concourse.

"The fair has probably finished," Alexander suggested.

"So soon and quickly?" Charlie asked. "That can't be."

They were approaching a wooden ladder running up the tunnel wall to a hatch.

"That must be the way!" Zoe exclaimed as she grabbed the ladder.

However, the cats were not so keen to exit the tunnel. Their deportment had become very unusual. They were lying flat on the floor of the tunnel growling and hissing as they looked straight up at the hatch. Their fangs were protruding from their mouths and their claws were extended and scraping along the tunnel floor. They were also gradually growing. It was almost as if something was behind the hatch door, and they were preparing for an assault.

Skadi moved forward and shoved Zoe to one side.

"Skadi!" Zoe exclaimed. "What's gotten into you."

But Skadi didn't even turn to look at Zoe. She was protecting her

Emissary.

She began climbing the ladder as the other cats followed her. Skadi lifted the hatch with her snout and proceeded cautiously as she squeezed herself through the hatch. She and the others were almost too big now to pass.

"It's night time up there." Charlie commented. "How can that be?" She looked at her watch. "We've only been down here for 10 minutes, and my watch says it's half past six. It should still be light outside."

The cats had all exited the tunnel and the group followed. They emerged into one of the old atriums at the centre of the building once filled with exotic plants from the world over but now empty and derelict.

The moon reflected through the old glass and lead dome overhead. Skadi and Freya were prowling up and down by the hatch but Parvati and Li-Shou had moved on up a stairwell which led to the mezzanine above.

The palace was still and silent. It didn't seem like a soul remained from the huge throng of people they had left behind them when they descended into the tunnel. A warm summer breeze filled the night air.

The group advanced and mounted the stairwell.

Zoe was still at the front. She was still filled with indignation and was looking for a confrontation to quell her anger. Shortly, she would not be disappointed. The group reached the top of the stairwell and found themselves on the mezzanine where Henry had stood in 1945.

The warm summer breeze was suddenly gone, and the temperature dropped rapidly.

The cats began growling and hissing again but this time with even more intensity. Parvati and Li-Shou had remained at ground level and were prowling back and forth along the verge of the hillside.

Freya and Skadi had climbed onto the top of the mezzanine balcony and stood guard. They knew what was coming and sensed it the moment they reached the hatch. A high-pitched ringing sounded from the hillside below as it rose up towards the palace.

Once again Tom went into a trance.

He was seeing through Henry's eyes that fateful night in 1945. Henry was desperately looking for something along the stone wall. Tom could see various carvings in the stonework which had been eroded by the elements over the years. They seemed to be Egyptian in origin.

The ringing sound grew as the cats moved back and forth hissing and growling ever more loudly. Zoe, Charlie, Stephen and Alexander held hands and planted the souls of the feet firmly on the stone floor of the mezzanine.

They all kept an eye on Tom who was moving quickly to the far end of the mezzanine.

Like Henry, Tom tripped and fell. Zoe let go of Charlie's hand and ran to assist him. By the time she had drawn close to him, his body was shaking violently, and he was convulsing as he reached out to the lifeless weather-worn carved image of Bastet.

Bastet was depicted with a female body and lioness's head.

She was the Egyptian goddess of cats, home, fertility and healing. However, she was more than that. She was the ultimate goddess of protection and the daughter of the sun god Ra. She was said to be the Eye of Ra (the all-seeing eye). She was a savage defender of the innocent and avenger of the wronged. She was both highly venerated and greatly feared. Despite her life promoting qualities, she was commonly known as 'the lady of dread' or the 'lady of slaughter'. She was not someone one would want to vex.

Her name was originally B'sst, then Ubaste, then Bast, then Bastet.

She was part of the Egyptian feline deities: Mau - the divine cat; Mafdet - Goddess of Justice; Sekhmet (daughter of Ra) -Goddess of War and Destruction; Mihos - God of Truth (son of Bastet); Pakhet - Goddess of Hunting.

Her cult centred at the city of Bubastis from at least the 5th century BCE.

Like many Egyptian deities, she acted as a guide to the dead in the afterlife.

Tom was reliving the death of Henry. Zoe put her hand on Tom's chest and was immediately repelled with such force that she toppled back and over the balcony edge.

Skadi had foresight like all great cats and had already run the length of the balcony wall making it just in time to grab Zoe's leg between her jaw and pull her back up.

The others rushed to Tom. There was no way that Tom could die like Henry, and he would not.

Tom could feel them smothering his entire body and face as they had Henry's. He had to stretch further and touch the carving.

Below, the ringing had reached a crescendo. They had risen to the top of the grass verge directly in front of the palace building.

Parvati and Li-Shou had grown to their full-size towering to a mighty ten feet. Skadi had jumped to the ground from the balcony to join Parvati and Li-Shou. The moment she hit the ground her body swelled to its full size also.

Freya remained with her Emissary Tom, lying by his side. She knew what was needed.

The four others said not a word. Instead, they held hands once more and this time their amulets radiated as did Tom's.

Tom knew it was now or never. They had engulfed him both inside and out. As they had killed Henry, they would eventually kill him. He thrust his arm as far as it could stretch and with the other arm he reached out to Freya.

His hands touched Bastet's head and Freya's at the same time amplifying the force.

The image of Bastet became perfectly defined in the stonework and then her form began to emerge from it and grow into a living being.

She stood as tall as the cats.

She looked at the group and at the grounds below. Then she looked down at Tom.

She took the aegis with its lioness head crowned by a sun disk and uraeus (a sacred serpent) from the golden thread cord around her waist and held it aloft with two hands, uttering but one word...

"Al-Mawt"

The cats roared so loudly that they could be heard for miles around as they reared up onto their hind legs.

Freya knew that Tom would be rid of these serpents with Bastet standing over him and she leapt onto the balcony wall and down to the ground below to join Parvati, Li-Shou and Skadi.

She grew as she moved so that by the time she attacked the serpents she was an impressive twelve feet tall. She was the largest of the cats.

The mist which had risen from the grass verge and that which covered Tom dissipated to reveal a bed of serpents. They were slithering over and around each other, intertwined so tightly it appeared they were a single form.

Then the serpents unlocked themselves and sprung up like coils. Their bodies hovered and swung in circles. Their mouths were open. Their fangs were poised to bite. Their forked tongues flicking in the air to sense their prey.

The cats ran and jumped headlong into the bed of serpents with their paws and claws flexed.

They lashed at the serpents cutting them to pieces as they advanced through the bed. As the serpents fell, their physical form turned to smoke and rose up into the night's sky.

Those serpents that had the opportunity to strike could not pierce the cats' skin. The cats were incredibly strong but the presence of Bastet and the additional deific power she bestowed on them made the cats indomitable. It was a massacre.

Bastet kneeled and touched Tom's chest with the palm of her hand. The serpents which covered his body vanished.

She spoke again but this time in English or at least that was how the group understood her.

"The followers of Apophis are seeking to return order to chaos and bring destruction, darkness and death to the living world. They must be stopped. This will assist you."

She took the necklace from around her neck and pushed out a stone. Although it was night time, the group could see every detail on the stone as though they were in bright daylight. The stone was an azur blue like nothing they had ever seen before. At its centre was a simply drawn eye with a black pupil.

"This was my father's and for now it is yours. I will collect it when your job is done," said Bastet. She paused and then continued. "And this belonged to your Society's Custodian. The followers of Apophis sought it the night of his demise."

She reached into a pocket in her robe and pulled out a scroll.

"He woke me with his dying breath, and I took it before the serpents could. It was too late for me to save him but not too late for me to create an illusion fooling the serpents into thinking they had taken the scroll. I will leave you now. The cats have finished their work."

Bastet handed the stone to Stephen and the scroll to Alexander.

With that she returned to being the weather worn carving in stonework of the balcony wall.

The cats were on the grass grounds below cleaning their paws and claws with great satisfaction.

In the distance, a very large murder of crows which had been roosting in the trees flew away squawking furiously.

Tom rose to his feet with Zoe and Charlie's assistance and brushed himself down.

"Are you feeling OK Tom? We were a little worried there for a second!" said Alexander.

"Just a second then Alexander... that's most comforting!" Tom said wryly.

"The girls were looking after you so well and then, of course, you had an Egyptian goddess by your side. Well, what could I add to that?" Alexander replied.

"If I'm not mistaken that was Bastet, one of the high Egyptian deities of protection," Stephen interjected. "I studied Egyptology at school. Apophis was an evil serpent god and nemesis of Ra - the sun god. Is this going to become any weirder?"

"I think it is," said Tom. "We should get moving. We need to find a place to study the scroll."

"There's something I need to check in the Great Hall first," Charlie said. "It's very important."

"We don't have time Charlie," replied Tom.

"I must," Charlie retorted. "I can't move on without it."

"We all need to stick together now. Things are becoming a little perilous to say the least!" said Alexander.

"Let her please, Tom," Zoe said. "She'll do it anyway, and as Alexander says, we need to stick together."

"Right then, let's get down there. What is it you want to look at anyway Charlie?" Tom enquired.

"It's Miss Tweedie," Charlie replied. "Something is not as it appears. I can't really say more than that. Something isn't right. I'll show you." Charlie said.

The group descended the stairwell to join the cats who had finished preening themselves and had returned to their normal size.

They made their way around to the Great Hall entrance. Naturally, the large blue doors were locked.

"Here you go," Alexander said as he raised his right hand pointing it at the middle of the door and turned it slowly to the right. The mortice bolt lock opened. Then Alexander raised his left hand and pointed it to the bottom of the door pointing his right hand to the top of the door. He pincered his thumbs and forefingers as if manipulating something and moved both hands slowly to the right. A clunk of the two huge door bolts could be heard falling open on the other side of the door.

"It's open. You can go in." Alexander said.

"Nice party trick!" said Zoe. "How did you do that?"

Alexander smiled. "I just willed it and well it happened."

"Yep," said Zoe. That's pretty much how it worked with me.

"Thanks Alexander," said Charlie as she moved cautiously towards the door.

"Hang on Charlie. We should go in with y..."

But before Tom could finish his sentence the door had swung open, and Charlie had been pulled inside with such ferocity that her body had contorted into a u-shape as she was dragged forward from her waste by an invisible force.

The large blue door slammed itself shut behind her.

CHAPTER 33

1945

Charlie came to an abrupt stop at the centre of the hall which was only lit by the moonlight shining through the windows. She could hear the very faint calls of the group outside and scratching of the cats at the door.

Alexander tried to open the door again as did the rest, but it wouldn't budge.

They all tried wrenching the doors off their hinges with their newly discovered power but not even that worked.

"Charlie!!!" screamed Zoe. "Charlie!!! Charlie!!!"

There was no reply. The group held hands and convened to full power with the cats and blew the doors to smithereens. After the dust settled, they walked inside the Great Hall, but it lay empty or at least that was how it appeared to them.

Charlie could hear the organ playing with a big band and the shuffling of people's feet as they danced around her. The sounds grew louder until men and women appeared arm in arm dancing and twirling around her in time with the music.

The ladies wore padded shoulders, nipped-in waist tops, A-line skirts which came down to the knee and peep-toe heels. Some women wore high-waisted wide flowing pleated trousers with loafers.

The men wore high-waisted flat front or single pleated straight trousers which were wide at the ankle with turn ups. They all wore spear pointed collar shirts with wide ties and V-neck short sleeve pullovers.

The mode and the music seemed reminiscent of the 1940s, but she was no expert.

At first, Charlie was concerned that these people were the Unremembered but soon realised there was a very different feel and look to her surroundings.

She wasn't experiencing muted echoes and images of the past. It was as if she were there living amongst these people in the Great Hall in the 1940s (or whenever it was).

Had she travelled back in time when she was pulled into the hall? Could these people see her? That question was quickly answered when a dashing young man took her gently by the hand and with the other hand swung her around and straight into a Lindy Hop. He soon realised that Charlie didn't know what to do as she stood almost motionless. So, he stopped dancing.

"Where have you been?" he said. "And what are you wearing? I have to say you look a little out of place. But… how presumptuous and rude of me! My name is Henry. I'm very pleased to meet you. I have to say you look ever so familiar. Have we met before?"

Charlie was struggling to catch up. It had to be said that of all the group, she had had the most frenetic few days and was quite exhausted despite her athletic physique and resilient nature. She hadn't said a word and could only muster a sweet smile before feeling very lightheaded and falling forward.

Henry stepped forward swiftly and caught Charlie in his arms cushioning her fall and bringing her gently to a lying position on the ground. Then he picked her up and took her outside to one of the benches on the concourse overlooking the city.

The night air had brought Charlie to.

"Wait here. I'll be right back. He walked over to a vending wagon parked on the concourse and wandered back proudly with a couple of ring-pull bottles of ginger beers.

"This is a bit of a treat," Henry said. "What with rationing. I know the owner. He has a little stash of pop. I hope you don't mind ginger beer. It has quite a particular taste. I thought it might give you a boost. Considering what you've been through."

Charlie spoke, "What do you mean... considering what I've been through?"

"Well, you know, Charlie. You're a little out of place... or time should I say?" Henry replied.

"Hang on a second... I didn't tell you my name." Charlie retorted anxiously.

"You didn't have to. I know where you've come from and what brought you here. I know who you are. And... please do not worry. I'm not here to harm you. Far from it. I'm here to protect you... to help you. I too am part of the Society. Well, not like you. I'm not an Emissary. I'm a Custodian."

"Did you say your name was Henry?" Charlie asked. She was still a little dazed from her blackout.

"Yes, that's right. Henry... Henry Waldly at your service."

"Waldly? But I know a Mr. Waldly. He... he too is a Custodian."

"Do you now? Well, what a small world it is then.

Henry was tall and thin with straight blonde hair. In fact, Charlie could easily see the likeness between Henry and the Mr. Waldly she knew.

"You saw something back then, didn't you?" Henry corrected himself. "I mean where you've come from… the future. 2010 or 2020, is it not?"

"How do you know?" Charlie enquired.

"This isn't the first time I've encountered one of the Society from outside my time… and hopefully it won't be the last!"

But what Henry did not know, and Charlie would soon come to realise, is that she would indeed be the last of the Society that Henry would meet in his lifetime. However, not before he would do her and the Society a great service.

"We'll have to wait until the evening is finished. It won't be long now."

The two sat and talked. Henry described his upbringing in the Yorkshire moors and explained how he came to be a Custodian and Charlie confessed how much she missed her beloved parents and recounted the exhausting tale of the last few days. She was just coming to the events at the palace immediately preceding her appearance in 1945 when Henry interjected saying,

"That's it. The band is packing up. Let's slip in and wait until everyone has gone."

Whilst the band was chatting to the security guards, Henry and Charlie tiptoed through the entrance and hid behind the large velvet armchairs which lined the walls of the Great Hall.

A few minutes later, they heard the last of the band members wishing the security guard good night and then the clunking of the door lock and bolts. The guard then switched out the lights and exited through an internal door which led to the adjoining annex of the palace.

Henry and Charlie both rose from behind the chairs and almost knocked heads in the darkness.

"Please excuse me," Henry said.

Charlie giggled in a rather childlike way. She had experienced an extremely intense and bizarre couple of days but felt very comfortable and relaxed in Henry's company. He was such a gentleman.

The moonlight shone through the stained-glass rose window above the doors of the Great Hall casting rays against the Henry Willis organ.

The organ had seen better days. A German 'doodlebug' bomb had exploded at the Southeast wall of the palace in 1944 and blown in the second rose window above it. It was exposed to the elements for several months before the hole in which the window was housed was finally covered by wooden boards.

Henry looked at his watch. "This is perfect timing," he said. The moonlight creates a marker against the organ."

"That's exactly what I wanted to investigate. I was introduced to a Custodian in my future. An old... well I'm not sure that's the word to describe her... a lady by the name of Miss Tweedie," Charlie stated.

"Ah, Miss Tweedie," replied Henry.

"You know her?" Charlie enquired.

"Oh, yes. She's a very mysterious individual. I know what you mean about age. No-one knows how old she is." Tom replied.

"I've seen her in photos across a century at least and she looks exactly the same in all of them. There were photos of her in an exhibition here at the palace in my future. There was one in particular where she is standing in the Great Hall after the fire which destroys the hall in the summer of 1980. She is inspecting the wall behind the organ." Charlie said.

"Another fire in 1980, you say?" Tom commented.

Henry and Charlie stepped up onto the stage and climbed the steps to the organ.

"Was she looking here?" Henry enquired. He pointed to an area where the moonlight struck the organ through the centre of the rose window above the main entrance.

"Yes, I think so," Charlie replied

"Ah, so she knew as well," Henry said.

"Knew what?" Charlie asked.

Henry pressed and pulled a series of stop knobs on the organ in a specific sequence until a small panel above the console popped open to reveal the bare wall behind it. He removed two loose bricks and then reached in. He produced two items.

The first looked very much like the scroll Charlie had seen

earlier. In that moment, she felt an enormous sense of anguish. She was so exhausted that she had not made the connection between the references Tom and Stephen had made to Henry the Custodian... and this Henry... the Custodian! She staggered a little but managed to steady herself and regain her composure.

Henry was preoccupied removing the second item and had not noticed Charlie's turn.

"Here we go," Henry said in a triumphant tone. "These are what Miss Tweedie was looking for."

He held both items in one hand and replaced the bricks and closed the panel with the other. Then he stepped down from the console.

Charlie tried hard to focus on his voice, but she could not rid her mind of the image of Tom on the balcony. And then, instead, she saw Henry engulfed by the serpents with his life ebbing away until he drew his last breath.

"Charlie, did you hear what I said?" Henry asked.

He could see her mind was elsewhere.

"Charlie, are you OK?" Henry enquired.

"I'm fine," Charlie replied.

Henry could see that she had been disturbed but knew better than to ask too many questions. Instinctively, he placed the items in his pockets and stepped towards her. He opened his arms out towards her. Charlie stepped forwards and welcomed his embrace. She placed her head on his shoulders and hugged him drawing her hands around his torso tightly.

Although it was Henry who had invited the embrace, he was taken by surprise by Charlie's reaction. He held her gently. He knew that he had broken protocol. Custodians were never to engage Emissaries in gestures of affection. Their role was only to assist and protect.

Charlie's emotions were laid bare. She had endured so much, too much. Tears rolled silently down her cheeks and onto Henry's shirt. There they stood together statuesque. Each could feel the beating of the other's heart.

Eventually, Charlie lifted her head from Henry's shoulder. Henry had already taken a pressed handkerchief from his breast pocket and passed it to Charlie who dabbed her eyes.

"Shall we sit down, and I will tell you about these?" He held up the scroll and a key in front of Charlie.

"Let's," Charlie replied softly. She knew that their time together would be short and precious.

First, Henry unravelled the scroll to reveal the map.

Charlie listened to him as he spoke of the Wiccan and the Wretched amassing a great army in a land hidden from the rest of the world. The map set out the path to that land.

Next, he spoke of the key. It was made of platinum, and it was difficult to tell which end was the bow and which end was the tip of the key. One end was in the form of an octagonal web and the other was in the form of a decagonal web. Both ends were about four centimetres in diameter. The blade was about twelve centimetres long and square.

No-one knew how old the key was or its exact origin. It was said to open a chest which stored a source of great power for the Emissaries.

As Henry spoke, Charlie felt the temperature in the air falling.

She interrupted Henry. "We need to leave this place now Henry," Charlie said in a decisive tone. Something is coming and it's very dangerous. I won't be able to stop it."

The temperature now began falling rapidly and mist floated under the far entrance doors. The moonlight which shone through the rose window faded as the night sky was covered by heavy black clouds.

Henry grabbed his jacket and put it on Charlie. Then Henry hugged Charlie for the last time. Unbeknownst to Charlie, Henry had placed the scroll and the key in the side pockets of his jacket.

He took Charlie's hand and led her to the small door which gave onto the annex adjacent to the Great Hall. He opened the door and said, "after you my dear."

He gestured for Charlie to pass through the doorway first. She smiled delicately and Henry tried to capture that image in his mind's eye. Charlie stepped through into the annex.

"We should head to the far side, over there in the corner. There is a small hatch which leads to the tunnel under the palace."

"OK," Charlie replied as she turned away from Henry and stepped towards the direction Henry had indicated.

That would be the last time they would see each other.

Charlie raced towards the hatch and heard the door slam behind her.

She turned to see Henry had not followed her. She stood momentarily and gazed towards the door. A tear ran down her cheek. Henry stood on the other side of the door. His hand still held the doorknob. He yearned to open the door and see Charlie's face again for one last time, but he knew that he must avoid the temptation. A tear ran down Henry's cheek.

Charlie turned again and ran towards the hatch.

Henry bent his head to wipe his cheek with the sleeve of his shirt. He looked down and, by his feet, lay the scroll which had tumbled from Henry's jacket pocket as Charlie passed through the doorway.

There was no time to go after Charlie. Henry's plan was to distract whatever lay in wait outside the palace so that Charlie could reach safety. He could contact the Society in his time once he had made his escape.

Henry picked up the scroll and buried it in his trouser pocket. He prepared himself, drew a deep breath and opened one of the main entrance doors. It was incredibly dark and foggy outside. The lamps along the concourse weren't working and the moon had been completely masked.

Henry could hear a ringing sound coming from the city below. At first, it was muffled but then grew very much louder. The combination of darkness and piercing noise was so disorienting that he lost his bearings entirely. He closed his eyes to focus, opened them and moved carefully along the palace wall... but alas, his fate was sealed.

Charlie had made her way through the hatch and into the tunnels beneath the palace. She could not stop thinking about Henry. She stopped in her tracks. Should she go back? Maybe she could save him? Where was she headed anyway? How was she going to return to her time?

She turned back and ran at lightning speed to the hatch. She scrambled into the annex and dashed across it to the side door which gave onto the Great Hall. She turned the knob but the door was locked.

Undeterred, Charlie took several paces back and charged the door, ramming it with the full force of her broad frame until eventually the wood cracked and the door flew open.

Without hesitation, she continued into the Great Hall and pulled open one of the large doors to the main entrance. Charlie froze... Tom, Zoe, Stephen and Alexander were standing before her.

She turned to look back into the Great Hall. Everything appeared as it had when she had walked in for the first time. The organ was nowhere to be seen.

Charlie turned back to the group.

"Did you see Henry? Where is he?" Charlie pleaded.

"Charlie," Tom said. "Henry died decades ago. Are you OK? Where did you go?"

Charlie's shoulders dropped and her head fell forwards. She shed one last tear, for from now on, Charlie would forever celebrate Henry's life and the love she had lost.
Zoe took Charlie gently by the arm and led her away. Zoe was developing a very strong bond with Charlie and could see the huge grief in her eyes.

"Did Henry give you his jacket? What a gentleman he must have been." Zoe said in a quiet and sympathetic tone.

Charlie lifted a lapel and could smell Henry's cologne as if he were there with her.

"He saved me, you know. I think we were here at the palace that night in 1945. He showed me a cachette in the Great Hall which hid a scroll and a key. I didn't have a chance to take a good look at them."

Stephen overheard Charlie.

"Did the scroll look like this?" Stephen asked. He showed the scroll to Charlie.

"Yes, exactly like that one." Charlie replied.

Charlie thought back to the moment she passed through the doorway from the Great Hall. The scroll had tumbled from the pocket of Henry's jacket which she was wearing. She had seen it hit the floor but had kept moving expecting Henry to pick it up and follow her. Henry must have planted it there when they hugged. She smiled at his ingenuity.

Had he given her the key as well? she wondered.

She padded the pockets of Henry's jacket and felt an imprint. She reached in and pulled out the key.

"My god!" she cried. "Call the others, Zoe." But they had already turned back to her.

The group had the map and the key.

The map was basic in design all apart from the very familiar and intricately drawn eight-pointed compass which lay at the centre of the scroll.

Below the compass in calligraphy was written *'Communicat Operibus Illius Malignis'*.

"God Speed," Alexander said. "That's a rough translation." He shrugged his shoulders.

Around the compass were drawn three islands - one to the west, one to the east and one to the south. To the north was drawn a ship. It resembled a square-rigged frigate.

The names of the islands were written across them: *'Lundy'* to the west, *'Palmyra'* to the east and *'Poveglia'* to the south.

Across the bow of the frigate was written *'H.M.S. Pearl'* and the words *'Bene Facitis Et Defendat'*.

Tom's arm began itching and instinctively he began to scratch it. The more he scratched, the more the itching intensified until it became a burning sensation.

"Ouch!" Tom yelped. He pulled up his sleeve to reveal the compass tattoo on his arm. The north point burned a bright orange.

"Bloody hell Tom. What is that?" Stephen said.

"Your tattoo Tom," Zoe said. "You've had it since the first day of school. Do you remember? You passed out at the school gates. That's the day we met Tramontane."

"We need to find the ship." Tom said. "I've been aboard her before. On the ocean during a battle."

"What do you mean Tom?" Alexander interjected. "That ship looks hundreds of years old. You can't have been aboard her. You're not making any sense."

"I know where she is." Tom said as he reached out for Zoe's and Charlie's hands who in turn reached out for Stephen's and Alexander's. The cats wove themselves into the middle of the commune. They all fell into a trance as the group's eyes shone yellow. Their bodies flickered and slowly faded until they vanished.

They were meant to reappear where Tom had envisaged - St. Mary's Church, Rotherhithe. The church was located near the bank of the Thames next to the old docks in Southwark, London... but they didn't.

Instead, they found themselves in a field beneath a huge yew tree next to a small church.

The group looked around for signs of where they were.

A few gravestones were spread around the ground among hundreds and hundreds of bluebells which stretched as far as the eye could see.

The girth of the tree trunk was at least ten metres. It must have been over a thousand years' old. Buried in the trunk was a crooked wooden door. It began to rattle and then swung open.

A young girl emerged but her form was incomplete and broken. She flickered in the sunlight as she struggled to move forward. Her mouth was moving. She was talking but the group could not hear what she was saying. In fact, there were no sounds around them at all. The leaves on the ground blew this way and that in the gentle breeze but did not rustle. The birds flew from the trees, but their wings did not flutter.

The girl continued to press forward towards the group as though she were struggling against a force which was pulling her back.

The group and the cats were transfixed as she drew ever closer. The cats did not make a sound. They did not feel threatened but knew they could not help.

Eventually, she was directly in front of Tom. She continued to talk but the group could hear nothing.

She was fading fast as her form became ever more transparent.

She dragged her arm up from her side and grabbed Tom's hand, prising it open. She lifted her other arm and opened her hand across Tom's palm as she finally succumbed to whatever she had been resisting.

Her form, which was now almost vaporous, was wrenched back through the doorway into the trunk of the tree. The door slammed shut and the silence ended as the leaves rustled and the birds fluttered above the group's heads.

Tom looked down at his palm. In it lay two keys. They were like the one Henry had given Charlie.

The next chapter in their story was about to begin and soon they would be united with the other three…

FIN

Copyright © - Dominic Fabian Danvers 2021

Printed in Great Britain
by Amazon